# Creepy

# Vampire Drive-iN

Ronnie Stich

ISBN: 0692608974
ISBN-13: 9780692608975

**Special Thanks**

Thanks to Sylvia Galan, Chris, and Luke for reading the book before it was released. I would also like to thank Joe Ocampo, Steven Juliano, Julian and Tamara Garcia, Tim Miller, Anja Contreras, and John Miorelli for their help and support.


Shawn, you are missed but not forgotten. I hope you enjoy being a vampire in this book.

For Luke.
Thank you for being so excited about reading this story.

# Chapter 1

Alicia's cell phone rang, as it always did, at the worst possible time. She was sprawled across her bed, her head in her hands, in the middle of an algebraic calculation—one she just couldn't figure out.

*Most annoying ringtone ever*, she thought to herself as she reached over a few scattered papers and an MP3 player to grab her phone from the nightstand.

"Hello?"

"Hey."

"Hi, Kathy. What's up?"

Kathy sighed. "Oh, not much. We just got back from a restaurant. My parents took me out for Italian food. They let me pick. What are you doing?"

Alicia twirled a mechanical pencil in her hands and frowned. "Math."

"Eww. Sorry."

"Yeah, I need help on it," Alicia admitted.

"How was the food? My parents never take us out to places like that anymore. Probably because of Jimmy." Her little brother had a reputation on certain sides of San Antonio. He was known as the screamer. Hated all foods that didn't have an abundance of chocolate chips in them, and so he screamed at all other foods ... especially Chinese food.

"You're not missing much," Kathy said nonchalantly. "Our waiter spilled some water on my dad—which was kinda funny, but my dad didn't think so."

"Oh." Alicia giggled.

"Then my steak was, like, medium and I asked for it well-done. You know?"

"Yeah," Alicia answered, envisioning how tender and juicy the steak must have been. "Medium's not bad, but you gotta get what you ordered."

"And my mom complained about the shrimp being too salty or too buttery or something, and I was, like, what's the big deal?" Kathy was talking so fast that she had to take a quick gasp of air before continuing. "And the guy at the table next to us was a loud-talker. Which is fine except that all he did was talk about taxes and investments. I hear enough of that stuff at home. And then the world was threatened by some weird aliens from another planet, and I ordered a piece of cheesecake."

Alicia thought on what she had just heard and felt a strange tingling sensation in her head. "Wait … *what*?"

"Cheesecake," Kathy replied with a fake laugh. "Yum. It's my favorite."

"Could you go back to the alien part, please?"

"Oh, yeah. No big deal," Kathy said before nervously clearing her throat. "Aunt Marilyn appeared, you know, materialized … so I snuck off to the bathroom with her, and she started telling me about a meeting she had with The Order."

The Mystical Order of Ghosts, Enigmas, and Cryptids—a powerful organization important to the existence and well-being of life forms everywhere. Located on the outer edges of another solar system, The Order exists in order to keep order. It not only helps to oversee, protect, and regulate the dimension Earth belongs to, but it also has ties to several other dimensions as well. Alicia shuddered at the thought of it. If The Order had a meeting about an alien threat to Earth, it was probably serious. Kathy's Aunt Marilyn—a ghost-aunt, mind you, now served as The Order's

Earth ambassador. As a former resident of Earth, her unique abilities to communicate with humans—both living and deceased—was an asset to The Order in many ways. As much as Alicia doubted, at times, the teenaged sanity of her best and closest friend Kathy, she completely trusted Kathy's amazing and talented Aunt Marilyn. She was the most interesting inter-dimensional ghost she had ever met. And she was quite a snappy dresser, too.

Kathy lowered her voice to say, "We need to have an emergency meeting."

She'd only joined The Ghost Friends chapter because Kathy hadn't given her much of a choice. At their weekly meetings, Alicia felt completely lost in discussions about creatures she'd never even heard of. "No ... I'm doing homework." She couldn't think of a better excuse. There was enough weirdness in her life, and whenever Kathy got them involved in something, the weirdness multiplied. "And I have to write a history paper."

"You're choosing math and history over saving the Earth?!"

"But it's about Abraham Lincoln."

Kathy let out a frustrated growl. "Ally, there won't be any more history, or math, or *anything* if we don't figure out how to handle this situation."

Alicia rolled over in her bed and cringed. "But I've been thinking about things ... life and stuff. I've decided I just wanna be a normal thirteen-year-old girl."

"What's *that* supposed to mean?"

"Well," Alicia began to explain with uncertainty, "I don't think I want to go to meetings anymore with The Ghost Friends chapter. I don't want to talk about ghosts or bigfoots or any other weird creatures. I mean, I agree that they deserve protection and the same rights and respect as the rest of us do, but—"

"But what?" Kathy interrupted.

"But it's kind of weird. Like, weirder than I thought it was going to be when I joined," Alicia admitted weakly. "Sorry."

"But *we're* the ones in danger this time, Ally."

Alicia thought on it, but remained silent.

"Okay. Cool," Kathy replied in a calm voice. "No big deal. We'll take care of it on our own ... *without* you."

Alicia felt horrible. "Are you mad at me?"

"No no no. It's cool. We'll figure it out. It would have been nice to have your help since you've seen some of this stuff before, but it's all right. I understand. It's a lot to handle at times. Talking to ghosts and other beings might be strange to you, but it's not to me."

"I'm sorry."

"I'll have to cancel the sleepover we had planned for next weekend though. Sorry."

There was a lump in Alicia's throat. "What?! But you said you weren't mad at me!"

"I'm not. It's just that the world will be over by then, so … you know. Maybe we can have a sleepover if we turn into ghosts or something after the world ends."

"Oh," was all that Alicia could think of to say.

"Yeah. So it was nice being your friend," Kathy said. "And I'll let Aunt Marilyn know that you're not going to help us save the Earth. She'll get over it. She might get a little upset that she's going to lose her job, what with the Earth being gone and all."

Alicia's eyes widened. "Oh no."

"What?"

"This is real isn't it?"

"Yes."

"I don't want Marilyn to lose her job with The Order."

Kathy waited in silence as Alicia thought about what to do.

"Okay, I'll help."

Kathy beamed with delight. "Awesome!"

"But are they yucky aliens?"

"Uh ... well ..." Kathy was afraid to answer.

"Do they have tentacles? Are they slimey? Do they eat people?" Alicia felt like she was about to hyperventilate just thinking about the many possibilities of grossness that these aliens might be.

"I don't know, maybe, sometimes, and I don't know."

Alicia's stomach felt weak.

"Look, don't worry. We've got The Order backing us up. All right?"

"Okay," Alicia answered robotically.

"Meet me in Mr. Walsh's classroom at lunch tomorrow. I'll get Marilyn to show up. And I swear ... if Mr. Walsh makes any of those kissy faces at Marilyn, I'm going to freak out!"

"Yeah. That's gross. Plus, he's a teacher and all."

"I gotta go," Kathy said. "I need to pick out an outfit for tomorrow."

Alicia was frozen with fear. A mixture of thoughts invaded her brain, almost all of them involving tentacled aliens that might want to eat her for trying to defend her planet.

"Don't worry, Ally. Finish your homework. Bye."

But it was too late. Alicia stared at the screen of the phone in her hand, her eyes blank and her mouth dry. She was terrified, worried, and just a little bit queasy. But she was kind of hungry as well. And as a teenaged girl, this sort of a distraction was very common.

*Hmmmm. I wonder if there's any of those chocolate-covered pretzels downstairs.*

But if Alicia had gone downstairs, looking for those chocolate-covered pretzels, she would have possibly seen something that she couldn't unsee. Because downstairs, standing alone in the dimly-lit kitchen, holding open the refrigerator door, was Alicia's dad, Mr. Harold Chavez. And he was hungrier than hungry ... he was *unnaturally* hungry. And he couldn't figure out why.

In the pit of his stomach was a strange rumbling, a craving for something that just couldn't be satisfied with anything from the inside of a human being's fridge. Harold Chavez eyed various cheeses, fruits, and yogurts ... clumsily pushed aside a head of lettuce and tipped over some milk. But the rumbling in his stomach was getting louder, becoming more intense. He slowly shut the refrigerator door, and then turned and stared blankly at the cupboards and the pantry door. There was nothing from inside the kitchen that would ease his craving. He realized in fear that his craving wasn't anything normal ... or human.

Harold's mouth began to tremble. He reached up to feel around his throat, and then further up for his chin. Harold then opened his mouth and carefully ran his fingers along the tips of his teeth. "What if I'm —?"

"Harold?" his wife Tina said softly.

This caused Harold to jump with a start, and he had to take a moment to catch his breath.

Tina stood at the entrance of the kitchen, clutching at her robe nervously as she eyed her husband with concern. "Are you all right?"

Harold shivered and twitched quite unnaturally. He then nodded and smiled as humanly as possible. "Yes, honey. I'm fang. I-I mean, *fine*. I'm fine."

# Chapter 2

Monday morning.

Mr. Walsh looked across the desk at Alicia with a smirk on his face. In the fluorescent lighting, his dark hair looked a little extra salted with grays that morning. He pulled a few fuzzy things off his dark-green sweater vest and pushed up his glasses. "The entire thing sounds a little far-fetched." With one eyebrow raised far above the other, he reached for his coffee mug before shaking his head. "*Aliens*?"

Alicia nodded in agreement, her green eyes looking greener than usual and her blonde hair shiny and straightened just perfectly with the new hair straightener she'd received as a gift from Kathy for Christmas. She'd become quite an expert with the new styling tool. And being that it was only mid-February, Alicia considered that to be a genuine accomplishment. "Exactly. It sounds a little crazy, doesn't it?" She then pointed at Kathy, seated in the chair next to her across from Mr. Walsh. "And just so you know, *she's* the one saying all of this, not me."

"Correction," Kathy replied with pouty pink lips and a perfectly manicured finger in the air. "Marilyn said it. The Order had a council meeting, and the threat from aliens was discussed."

And so logically, The Ghost Friends chapter, which consisted of only three members—Kathy, Alicia, and their English instructor, Mr. Walsh— would be The Order's point of contact. And even though their chapter dealt mostly with ghosts and solving ghostly issues, The Ghost Friends chapter didn't discriminate. They had made an agreement with The Order to help with any issues deemed out-of-the-ordinary for most humans to handle. Whether it be a depressed ghost in need of a pep talk, or a goblin in search of a forest relocation ... The Ghost Friends chapter was ready to help. However, this was a much different sort of situation ...

Mr. Walsh leaned forward and placed his elbows on the edge of his desk. "Aliens, huh? How credible is The Order's source?"

"Their *what?*" Kathy asked, flashing her deep blue eyes at him in confusion.

Mr. Walsh explained, "How reliable is the information? How well do they trust the person, persons ... or creatures, The Order obtained the information from?"

"Well," Kathy began in all seriousness, "we're talking about The Order here. I'm sure they wouldn't have Marilyn passing this sort of thing on to our chapter if it wasn't true."

"All right," Mr. Walsh said with both hands held out in front of him. "I'm just a little confused. That's all."

Alicia rolled her eyes. "I don't blame you. It's not a lot to go on."

Kathy turned to study Alicia's face. "What do you mean by *that*?"

"You haven't really told us much of anything," Alicia explained. "You told us that aliens have threatened Earth. Then you said that the threat will be carried out by Saturday ... and that these aliens are really, really strange."

"They *are* strange," Kathy replied quietly, but then smiled to herself. "But, like, in a cool way. Wait until you find out."

Alicia eyed her carefully. "What does that mean?"

Kathy only shrugged and raised her eyebrows, knowingly.

Mr. Walsh leaned forward. "That's all the information you have?"

"For now," Kathy said, tossing her dark hair behind her shoulder, doing her best to cover-up that she actually did know more than she was saying.

Mr. Walsh sighed one of those grown-up kind of sighs. "It's all a little hard to believe."

"Totally," Alicia added.

Kathy crossed her arms and sank into her seat. "I wish Marilyn was here. She'll explain things."

"Where is she?" Alicia asked.

"Scotland. Dealing with some castle haunting."

Mr. Walsh smiled warmly. "She really is a great lady."

Kathy and Alicia glanced at each other. Alicia covered her mouth to hide a large grin.

"It's not funny," Kathy hissed at her.

"Yes, it is."

Suddenly, there was a crackling sound in the back corner of the room. Mr. Walsh spun around in his seat as the girls watched and waited, wide-eyed. An electrical energy filled the room. Kathy quickly turned and ran for the door, checking to make sure that no other students would try to enter the classroom. And next to a poster about proper comma usage, Marilyn started to appear.

First to materialize were her legs and arms, and then her perfect chocolaty brown hair. Marilyn's beautiful face soon followed, and then the rest of her. A misty cloud swirled in the air around her, causing Marilyn to cough and wave her hands in front of her face.

Kathy ran towards her. "Are you all right, Marilyn?"

"Yes, of course." She coughed again, lightly and delicately. She pulled at her blouse. "I don't think polyester travels well in between worlds. Or perhaps it's my new ghost-glam hairspray."

Mr. Walsh jumped up from his seat, knocking over a cup of pens on his desk. "Uh, hello, Marilyn."

Marilyn fluttered her eyes at him in return. "Hello, Johnny."

"Johnny?!" Kathy asked in disgust. She grabbed onto Marilyn's arm. "No no no. We don't have time for hellos or anything like that. Let's just get down to business."

Kathy then quickly walked her aunt past Mr. Walsh's desk and offered her the seat next to Alicia. Marilyn blushed and smiled at Mr. Walsh before sitting down. Quite annoyed, Kathy grabbed another chair and pulled it across the floor, making a lot of noise in the process before placing it next to her aunt.

Kathy plunked herself down and fixed a serious gaze upon Marilyn. "What more did you find out?"

Marilyn tightened her red lips and began to play with a lock of her hair. "Not very much, unfortunately."

Mr. Walsh frowned. "So it's true? The whole alien thing?"

"Yes." Marilyn now looked completely distressed. "I don't know what more to tell you. These are very selfish aliens. They come from a planet called Vashmirain, and their name is too ancient and too difficult to pronounce, so we just refer to them as Vashmirians ... or space vampires."

Kathy sprang out of her seat. "YES! See?! Vampires! Finally! Isn't this exciting?! I couldn't wait for you guys to find out!"

"Vampires?" Mr. Walsh's mouth dropped open. "That doesn't sound very good."

"No, it's not," Marilyn agreed. "They're just awful. And they're very angry at Earth, for some reason. We just can't figure out why."

Kathy, doing her best to contain her excitement, tapped her fingers excitedly on Mr. Walsh's desk. "Okay. I'm sorry, but this is completely awesome.

Why isn't anyone else excited about this?"

"Kathryn," Marilyn began, "believe me, dear. There's really nothing to be excited about."

Alicia looked as if she was about the cry. "They're probably horrible, nasty creatures that don't look anything like the vampires we see in the movies, Kathy."

"Actually," Marilyn interjected. "They do look like the vampires from the movies—the old 1950s movies. Exactly like them."

"Really?!" Kathy exclaimed.

Marilyn sighed. "Unfortunately, yes. Black capes, pale faces, creepy voices—"

"Do they sleep in coffins?"

"Yes."

Kathy smiled the biggest, toothiest smile that any of them had ever seen.

"Oh, Kathy," Marilyn said. "I really do wish you'd see the bigger picture here. They want to destroy us."

"But why?" Mr. Walsh asked.

"We just don't know, Jonathan." Marilyn answered honestly. "I wish we did. And that's why we need your help. If we could find out what they're so angry about, maybe we could stop them. We do think that their first target will be here in San Antonio."

"But what can we do?" Alicia asked timidly. "You said they're going to destroy the world by Saturday. Kathy and I were going to make brownies and go to the mall that day."

Marilyn leaned over and patted her shoulder. "Now, dear. You listen to me. These nasty, ancient vampires aren't going to destroy Earth. We simply won't let them."

"Besides, they could be bluffing," Kathy added optimistically, almost as if she was taking the vampires' side.

Marilyn nodded cautiously. "Yes, there's a slight chance, very slight, that they are bluffing. At least I hope so."

Mr. Walsh rose slowly from his seat, pushed up his thin-framed glasses, and proudly raised his chin into the air. "No space vampires are going to destroy my planet. Not while I'm an English teacher at Sinatra Middle School! Because it's my job ... no, no ... *my duty* as a human being to protect and defend this planet against these disrespectful creatures of the night! And if they think for one second that they can just show up here in their spaceships—"

"They drive hot rods, sweetie," Marilyn corrected him. "So they'll probably arrive in one of their big garage-ships."

"T-They what?"

"Oh yes. They're quite a snazzy bunch of ghouls."

Mr. Walsh sat back down. "Oh. Okay."

Kathy shook her head in awe. "This is going to be the coolest week of my life."

# Chapter 3

Alicia sat on a bench outside the school, waiting for her father to pick her up. Early February was still cold in Texas, but not unbearably so. Alicia liked the way the cool wind felt on the tip of her nose. In fact, she liked it so much that she almost forgot how late her father was until her phone started to vibrate inside her book bag.

It was a text message from Kathy asking, "Has he picked you up yet?"

Alicia hesitated to answer, "No." She knew what Kathy's response would be.

"Need a ride?"

"No thanks."

But Kathy wasn't the type to let things go that easily. "You ok?"

Alicia stared out across the parking lot and watched as some of the teachers were beginning to pack things into their vehicles. Evil school things like lesson plans and binders filled with ideas meant to ruin kids' lives ...

"My dad's acting strange," she typed, not sure if she should send it. That was the type of text that would trigger several questions from Kathy because she was very much like a forensic investigator. Of course in this situation, it would be called "being a good friend." Kathy would most definitely go into therapist mode with a text like that. But Alicia risked it, and pressed send.

It took only seconds for Kathy's response. "I'm sorry. Parents are crazy. What's happening? Is there anything I can do to help?"

Alicia smiled and looked around as her father's car pulled up. "He's here," she typed quickly, then slid her phone back into the front pocket of her bag, zipping it shut. She quickly gathered her things: her book bag, a water bottle, and a notebook that didn't fit inside the book bag, and rushed up to her father's dented red sedan.

"Hey there, Ally," her father said as she climbed inside. "Sorry I'm late. This project at work has been a real pain."

"Ug." Alicia shook her head. "I don't want to talk about projects. I have one due soon. Haven't even started."

"How was school today?"

Alicia knew not to give too many details. A normal day at school was all he needed to hear about. "It was fine."

"Did you turn in that paper on Lincoln?"

"Yes."

"Oh, good."

Alicia turned to look out her window, feeling the next part of the conversation coming, a part she just didn't want to get into. In the silence, she turned toward the window, closed her eyes, and hoped that she was in the clear, that he might have been too busy at work to remember, or that the project he was working on had scrambled up his mind a bit ...

"Ally, I know I haven't been home a lot lately. I miss hearing about you and your life at school. Is there a boyfriend I should know about or anything?"

*Nooooooo!*

"I've been getting stuck at work more than I'd like to be. And I get up earlier than usual to go into work early. I know it's been a lot for you guys to deal with at home."

"Yeah. It's okay, Dad," she replied. "There's nothing new going on. Everything's the same at school. No boyfriend." *Yuck.*

"It's just this project at work," her father

continued, "I think it's ... doing something to me. I don't know how to explain it, and I know how crazy that sounds."

Alicia didn't want to look at him because she didn't know how to react. But she knew she had to say something, and she was certain that jumping out of a moving car wasn't an option. "What do you mean, Dad? Like it's hurting your eyes or something? Mom says you don't wear your glasses enough. Are you on the computer a lot?"

"It's the software. The program I've been working on. It's for this really important client in California. Like a restoration type of thing," he explained with a distant look in his eyes. "I work on it all day and sometimes at night at the house when you guys are all asleep. I'm always working on it. There's a deadline. A due date. You understand?"

"Yes." Alicia thought about it. Her father had been acting a little different lately. It wasn't too bad, at least not as bad as he was making it out to be. He did pace around the house a lot late at night, and always around the time she wanted to sneak into the kitchen for a late night snack.

"I guess what I'm trying to say is that I'm fine. It's just this project at work. It's making me a little bit kooky. That's all." Alicia's father then let out one of those unbalanced laughs that she'd only seen on TV—the kind that villains would do in cartoons.

"Uh," Alicia replied after a slight pause. "It's okay, Dad. You don't have to explain anything to me about work." She tried to think of a way to change the subject. A topic like dinner might be more interesting. Unless they were having leftovers ... nobody wants to talk about leftovers.

Alicia's father slowed the car at a stop sign and stared past it with glassy eyes. "I need a vacation. Or maybe a new car," he said in a monotone voice.

Alicia turned to him and squinted her eyes. "Wouldn't mom get upset if you got a new car?"

But her father just sat there, both of his hands clutching the steering wheel, looking straight ahead, his face expressionless. "Like a fast car. Something loud."

"Dad?" she said with concern. "You can go. The stop sign is ... done now."

"Huh? Oh," he realized with a start. "Sorry, sweetie."

Alicia smiled and then discreetly turned to face the window again. She unzipped the front pocket of her book bag and pulled out her phone, contemplating exactly how to text what she wanted to text to Kathy without making it sound over-dramatic.

So she typed, "Kathy, my dad is POSSESSED, and I am VERY afraid. PLEASE don't cancel our sleepover because of aliens. I need to get away from him this weekend!"

# Chapter 4

The next day.

Lunch. Not the best time to discuss things that you don't want other kids to hear about. But when else are you going to get the chance to discuss things that need to be discussed? Especially urgent things like canceled sleepovers and crazy dads? Alicia didn't feel like she had a choice. These were urgent matters. She was just going to have to be careful about how she went about it around so many other eighth graders.

Kathy set her paper bagged lunch next to Alicia's tray and smiled. "Slop again, huh?"

"I happen to like the pizza here," Alicia replied.

"Oh. Is that what that is?"

Alicia faked a smile. "Ha ha. So very funny, Miss Preston." She glanced around the cafeteria and lowered her voice a little. "Sit down. We have important things to talk about."

Kathy whisked away some chunks of food that had been left on the seat. "Trust me. I know we have things to discuss. Where's Beth?"

Alicia nodded. "Her mom checked her out early today for a doctor's appointment."

"Okay, good." Kathy said. "I mean, not because I want her to be sick or anything, but you know what I mean. We can't have her listening to what we say."

"I agree. It's too embarrassing."

Kathy scrunched up her face. "What are you talking about? She's going to figure it out one day soon anyway. You disappear once a week for meetings, and she's usually texting you the whole time asking you where you are, and if you want to talk about boys—"

"What?"

"*What* what?"

"What are you talking about?" Alicia asked.

"The Ghost Friends. Bethany still doesn't know about your membership, right?"

"No, she doesn't. But I'm not talking about that." Alicia was now seriously frustrated. "I'm talking about my dad. *He's* embarrassing. He's been acting really strange, and I think he's living a secret double life!"

Their lunch table, and the ones next to it, went

quiet as Alicia realized how loud her voice had become. Kids, some with food hanging out of their mouths, were now staring.

"Way to go, Ally." Kathy snickered.

Alicia put her head into her hands and sighed.

Kathy glared at a few boys and then opened her lunch. "Alright. Tell me what's going on ... *quietly*."

With some doubt about how to begin, Alicia poked a finger at the slice of pizza on her tray. It seemed a lot less appealing to her than it had been just moments earlier. And a lot soggier, too. "He stays up all night working on a project for work. Once, last week, he even left the house at, like, three in the morning. At dinner, when my mom asked him where he'd gone, he said he went into work early."

"Five hours early?"

"Yeah."

"Sorry," Kathy said while shaking her head. "That is strange."

Alicia looked at her with a most serious look on her face. One Kathy hadn't seen since Alicia had accidentally worn two different colored socks to school. "Your dad is his boss."

Kathy nodded.

"Do you think he knows anything about this

stuff?"

"I don't know, Ally. My dad might run the show over there, but I never hear him talking about any of the computer guys. He's more interested in the products they make—not their personal lives."

Alicia frowned.

"There are a lot of people working there."

"Could you at least ask him?"

Kathy looked away from her nervously. "I guess so."

Alicia let out a shaky breath. "He's changed, Kathy. He's like some zombie creature from the computer programming lagoon. I need your help. I need to know what's going on."

"I'll see what I can find out, but I can't promise anything." Kathy paused for a second and tried not to laugh. "My dad still calls your dad Charlie."

"What? His name's Harold."

"Well, I know that. But do you see what I mean? If he doesn't know his name, how's he gonna know what's making him crazy?"

Alicia's hopes were now sinking. In her eyes, Kathy's dad was the answer. He just had to know something about what was going on.

"I'll do my best, Ally," Kathy tried to assure her. "So do you mind if we talk about the end of the world now?"

Alicia rolled her eyes. "Do we have to? I'm kind of upset about my dad."

"I can't have a sleepover at my house if space vampires are coming to Earth, Ally."

"Can we talk about it after you try to find out what's going on with my dad?" Alicia's eyes were large and desperate. They reminded Kathy of a cute stuffed animal with over-sized eyes she had sitting on a shelf in her room. The doll always looked like it needed a hug ... or maybe some smaller, less depressing eyes.

Kathy pulled out her phone and tapped on the screen until she was staring at a calendar. She let out an exaggerated breath. "Let's see ... it's Tuesday. End of the world is possibly on Friday ... hmmm. It's going to be kind of a rush deal, but okay."

"Thanks! I owe you, Kathy!"

Without warning, the school's speaker system crackled to life above their heads.

"*Attention Sinatra Middle School students. Please, don't forget about family movie night, this Friday at the old City Drive-in movie theater. This special movie night will be hosted by the student council and The Piranhas car club. Bring your families out for some fun, and be sure to wear your 1950s clothing.*"

Alicia looked at Kathy for her reaction, but she was too busy opening a granola bar and seemed totally disinterested in the announcement.

*"And to stay true to the 1950s theme for the night, the movie being presented will be a super scary, black-and-white creature feature entitled, Condemned Vampire Cookout. Bwahahahaha!"*

Kathy's face instantly lit up.

"Have you ever heard of that movie?" Alicia asked her. Kathy knew more about classic monster movies than any kid or adult she'd ever met.

She seemed almost insulted by the question. "No," she answered with a rather twisted look in her eyes. "Actually, I haven't."

Alicia frowned. "Well, it sounds dumb and I don't have any 1950s clothes anyway."

*"So tell your parents and come by the office to pick up a flyer for more info. And don't worry students … the movie is safe for all ages, so bring your little brothers and sisters, too!"*

"Great," Alicia grumbled.

"I'm going!" Kathy declared as she slammed her fist on the table and bit into her healthy treat.

"I figured you would."

"Yeah," she replied with a mouth full of granola bits. "End uf duh werld and all. Might af well go owt in style. Monsfer mofees rule!"

# Chapter 5

Kathy watched her father in the kitchen of their home. He was staring down at a plate of frozen strawberries with a fairly serious look on his face, a look too serious for strawberries. He was still in his work clothes: a nice button up cream-colored shirt, dark-brown slacks, his tie was gone, probably draped over his favorite arm chair in the living room. Kathy twisted her lips and crossed her arms.

"They'll never defrost," her father said.

"Put them in the microwave," Kathy suggested.

"They'll get squishy." He turned to her and smiled. "What are you doing down here, honey? You don't have any homework tonight?"

Kathy nodded proudly. "I completed everything in class."

"Oh, okay." Her father smiled. "You look like you have something on your mind."

"I do," she admitted.

"Well, since these strawberries are never going to defrost, I have some time to talk."

Kathy decided to take a seat on a stool next to the countertop. And even though she stared at the strawberries with great interest, she had her mind on other things—many other things. Like how she should have been up in her room searching the Internet for any recent flying saucer sightings, or more specifically … any recent cases of vampire attacks.

"So what's on your mind?" her dad asked, snapping her out of a daze.

"Oh. Right. … um … it's Alicia," Kathy answered. "She's worried about her dad."

"Charlie Chavez?"

"No, Dad. His name's Harold."

Kathy's father tilted his head in confusion. "Harold? Ah … that's right. But his nickname's Charlie."

"No, it isn't." Kathy shook her head. "Anyway, Ally says her dad's been working a lot. You know? A little too much."

"Well, good for him!" her father declared proudly.

"No, Dad. Ally's worried. She says her dad's changed."

Kathy's father looked into his daughter's eyes,

feeling that something wasn't right. "Changed?"

"Yes, but I told Ally it wasn't any of my business to ask you anything," she said with sad eyes. "But she's my friend."

"I understand," he replied. "And you sound like a very good friend."

What he said embarrassed her, but it was certainly true. Still, she tried not to smile.

"Adults act differently sometimes when they're working on important projects. And if I remember correctly, Mr. Chavez is working on something pretty special. In fact, I think it's something fun!"

"Fun?" This piqued Kathy's interest. She had never heard of work being called fun before.

"Yes. A very important client of ours collects old, obscure films from Hollywood. He asked if I knew anyone that could help restore some of them. Then, he wants them saved in a newer, more modern format. Digital."

Kathy nodded. "He wants his old films run through some program on a computer that makes them look better, right?"

"Yes," her father answered. "And then saved for later so he can watch them when he likes — without damaging the old film reels they came from originally."

"Oh. Yeah, I've heard of that."

"Mr. Chavez is helping."

Kathy thought on her next question carefully. "Dad?"

"Yes, Kathy?"

"Would that make a guy go crazy?"

Her father tipped his head back in laughter. "Well, I'm sure some of the films are pretty bad — not very well done, I mean. Mr. Fuller, the client, collects some pretty interesting old science fiction films. Usually, they're the ones most people have forgotten about. That's what makes them so special. They call them B-movies, low-budget stuff."

Kathy sat straight up in her seat. She knew quite well what B-movies were. And in some of them, she could see the zippers on the backs of the actors' monster costumes. "That does seem interesting."

"Yes, well," her father chuckled before continuing, "Mr. Fuller sure thinks they are. But, I guess I could see how watching them over and over might make a guy go a bit loco."

"Oh, Dad. You can't tell Mr. Chavez what I said about him. Ally told me in confidence. I want her to trust me."

Kathy's father grinned warmly at her and then looked at the frozen strawberries on the plate in front of him. "Don't worry, honey. I'm sure Mr. Chavez is fine. I'm not going to say anything to him. I only see him when he waves at me from the driveway after dropping Ally off at the house."

"Okay. Thanks, Dad."

"That reminds me. Have you been planning that sleepover for this weekend? You need to make a list of goodies for us to buy from the store before Saturday."

Kathy grabbed a strawberry from the plate and tapped it on the side of the counter. It was still as hard as a rock. "That's okay, Dad. I didn't want to tell you this, but ... there might not be a Saturday anyway."

Her father looked sideways at her. "Why not?"

"I can't really tell you. But I can promise that I'm doing everything I can to stop it from happening."

"To stop *what* from happening?"

"The vampires." Kathy's eyes widened. "Oops!"

"Okay," her father said apprehensively. "I hope your Aunt Marilyn doesn't have anything to do with this."

Kathy sat silent and still.

"Make your junk food list anyway," her dad said as he pushed the plate of berries to a spot in front of Kathy, giving up on them entirely. "And tell Ally her dad will be fine. The project he's working on will be over by Thursday. That's only two more days."

"Okay, Dad," Kathy replied before realizing something incredible. Something she couldn't believe she hadn't realized before—Alicia's dad was probably watching the coolest, cheesiest science fiction films ever made. And Alicia had no idea how high her dad's coolness points had gone up because of it. To Kathy, it was mind-boggling. "Wow," she whispered to herself as her father exited the kitchen.

# Chapter 6

Wednesday. After school.

Alicia sat at the top of the bleachers, staring into a distant sea of football practice uniforms, angry coaches, and all kinds of sports clutter and gear that she wasn't really familiar with. It was chilly outside. A nice sort of chilly that had Alicia pulling the sleeves of her jacket over her hands. The soft wind blew through her hair, and if Alicia had looked into the compact mirror she had stored inside her book bag, she'd see that her cheeks and nose had gone rosy.

She was supposed to be paying attention, writing an article on something—anything for her journalism class. But there were too many distractions prying her away from her task. The fluffy gray clouds, the scribble drawings she kept scribbling at the top corner of her notebook, and some kid next to her that was smacking loudly on a mouth full of bubble gum.

*Why in the world did I choose to write about football?* Alicia wondered, her eyes drifting off into the sky. There were a million other things to write about: the local animal shelter, the epidemic of food fights in the school cafeteria, homework rage, or how to get a college scholarship ... things like that would have made for a very informative article. Football was just too ... football-ish. She didn't even understand how the game was played. And as Alicia second-guessed her topic of choice, Kathy appeared at the bottom of the bleachers and waved.

Alicia smiled excitedly. As Kathy made her way up the bleachers, clomping and stomping in an amazing pair of black leather boots—designer, no less—she kindly took the time to acknowledge other students along the way. Kathy was pretty cool like that, and it was quite a change from just months ago when Kathy was still new to Sinatra. Now, she was already considered very popular. Alicia felt lucky to be her friend. Under strange and uncommon circumstances in the beginning, but it didn't really matter how they'd become friends, it only mattered that they were friends now. And that made Alicia very happy.

"What's going on?" Kathy asked. She glanced

over at the gum-chewing kid for a second. "Someone told me you were up here watching the team practice. I didn't believe it at first, but here you are. You sick or somethin'?"

Alicia laughed. "No. It's for an article. One of those fake newspaper things for journalism."

"Ohhhhh," Kathy replied with a nod. "Well, do you mind if I sit with you guys?"

Alicia looked at the kid next to her. "I'm not *with* him. He's just … here."

The kid, a scruffy dark-haired boy in a plain T-shirt and black jeans, reacted with a surprised look on his face before scooting away just enough for Kathy to take her place in between them.

Kathy then leaned in close to Alicia and said, "I got some info on your dad."

Alicia gasped. "You do?!"

"Yes. But we can't discuss it next to this guy," Kathy insisted, pointing next to her.

"I can hear you," the scruffy boy said.

Kathy giggled. "Sorry." She turned to him, smiled her charming smile, and shrugged her shoulders at him apologetically.

The boy gathered up his water bottle and backpack, and then blew an extra-large pink bubble at them until it popped with a nice clean bang. He scooted farther away from them, glaring at Kathy as he did.

"Yikes," Kathy whispered to Alicia with a cautious smile on her face. "That kid's scary."

"What about my dad?" Alicia reminded her anxiously. She had a crazed look on her face—the kind that meant business. Serious business.

Kathy felt a bit uncomfortable. "My dad didn't say much, but it's something."

"What did he say?!"

"To make a long story short," Kathy began, "your dad's working on a really cool project. He's the luckiest guy at McDaniels, Daniels and Sons Technologies."

Alicia's face hardened. In her eyes sat a mixture of confusion and something that looked like anger. "What are you talking about? Whatever he's working on is making him crazy!"

"Well, your dad must be really good at what he does over there, because my dad says that this project is special." Kathy raised an eyebrow. "And it has a connection to Hollywood."

"What do you mean?"

The loud pop of a bubblegum bubble startled them, causing both girls to jump. Kathy quickly spun around and stared into the boy's face. He was obviously quite interested in what they were discussing. "I'm sorry. This conversation is private, and you're sitting just a little too close."

The boy creased his forehead and then scooted back a few more inches, his dark eyes fixated on Kathy's face.

Kathy turned back to Alicia. "Anyways," she said with a careful, low voice. "There's this big important client that my dad's worked with that lives in California. He's really into old Hollywood movies. Like, the *really* old ones. Black-and-white!"

"Okay," Alicia replied.

"So he asked my dad if he knew anyone that could fix the old movies he found — they're the kinds on film reels!" Kathy's entire face was alive with excitement, her blue eyes sparkling.

"My dad is the one fixing the films?"

"Yeah!" Kathy burst out.

Alicia looked a little dazed out as she tried to picture the process in her head. "Oh. Okay."

"Your dad's probably acting all messed up because he's been watching amazing, cool old movies that no one else has seen in years! That kind of thing can mess with your head because the coolness level is through the roof!"

Alicia sighed, still concerned. "Maybe that's it. He's not really into old movies. So maybe he's just annoyed."

"*Annoyed*?!" Kathy asked in shock. "How could he be annoyed? Some of those movies are old science fiction pictures ... ones that the world has forgotten about! Your dad is part of a historical experience beyond words!"

"Okay, calm down, Kathy." Alicia laughed.

And then the boy with the dark eyes said, in an eerie, peculiar voice, "I think it's cool."

Kathy turned to face him. "You like old movies?"

"Maybe," he said as he whisked away a few strands of hair from his face.

"How about science fiction films?"

"I *especially* love science fiction films," he answered with confidence.

Alicia scooted in closer and leaned over Kathy. "Are you going to the old drive-in on Friday for movie night? They're showing an old science fiction movie."

The boy grinned wide. "Of course. I wouldn't miss it for the world. Are you two going?"

Alicia started shaking her head. "I don't really—"

"I am," Kathy interrupted her to say.

The boy watched as the football team formed into a line on the field. "Funny how you two were talking about restoring old movies that haven't been seen in, like, forever."

"Why's that?" Kathy asked.

"Because the movie they're planning to show at the drive-in on Friday hasn't been seen in a theater … ever."

"Ever?"

"*Ever.*"

"That's impossible," Kathy declared adamantly.

"Is it?" the boy asked. He then eyed Alicia. "Maybe you should ask her father about it."

Kathy's and Alicia's eyes nearly popped out of their heads as they started to make the connection. Kathy turned and grabbed onto Alicia's shoulders. "It's Condemned Vampire Cookout! I knew there was something strange going on with that film! It's not listed anywhere online!"

Alicia asked, "But why would they show it to our school? It doesn't make any sense!"

Both girls turned to get a reaction from the dark-haired boy seated next to them … but he was gone.

Alicia felt a bit faint as she watched the blur that she thought most resembled Kathy, jump up from her seat to scan the bleachers. She could then hear Kathy ask frantically, "Where'd he go?!"

Alicia closed her notebook and shook her head in disbelief. "I don't know, but I know one thing."

"What's that?"

"Condemned Vampire Cookout made my dad go crazy. I'm not going to the drive-in on Friday."

"Come on, Ally!" Kathy begged. "We have to go!"

"Something really weird is happening," Alicia said robotically. "And I think we need to have another chapter meeting to discuss it with an adult. Maybe we should get some advice."

"Okay. I'll contact Marilyn tonight."

"Yes," Alicia replied in a spacy voice. "You do that, Kathy. And you do that soon because I think something really bad is happening here. Something really really really really really bad."

Kathy gasped. "I know ... the movie ... your dad ..."

Alicia nodded.

"I think he's working with the space vampires!"

# Chapter 7

Wednesday evening.

"**I** am very disappointed that the two of you spoke about chapter business in front of another human," Marilyn huffed while placing a hand on her hip.

"But we weren't talking about chapter business," Kathy said in their defense. "We were talking about Ally's dad!"

Alicia decided that it was her turn to jump in. "We didn't know it had anything to do with ... well, *anything* ... until that boy said something about the school movie night."

Marilyn stared at them in silence, expressionless. The three of them were on the front porch of Alicia's home, waiting for her father to return from a long day at work. He stayed late and said he'd be home around seven. Kathy had taken his place at the dinner table that evening, which gave Jimmy, Alicia's younger brother, many opportunities to call her Mr. Harold. "Mr. Harold, can you pass me the salt," this and "Mr. Harold, please tell me how your day at work went," that. Jimmy was full of his kindergarten jokes. But of course, Alicia and Kathy didn't find any of them very entertaining. Kathy, trying her best to be an excellent guest, did fake a few laughs for Jimmy, but it was difficult. She'd only stayed for dinner to have a chance to see Alicia's dad as soon as he arrived home. She wanted to see for herself how strange he was acting.

"That's why we wanted to have a talk with you, Auntie," Kathy said to Marilyn. "We think we've figured something out."

"Yes," Alicia agreed. "We're not exactly sure what we've figured out, but we think it's something to do with those vampires."

Just then, a car pulled into the driveway—it was Alicia's dad.

Kathy put on her most serious expression, careful to erase anything that might give away what they'd been discussing. "Everyone act natural."

Marilyn frowned. "But I'm supernatural!"

"He can't see her anyway, Kathy!" Alicia reminded her.

"Oh yeah! I forgot! He doesn't believe in stuff like that!"

Alicia looked back at Marilyn, making sure she wasn't offended. "I guess you could say it like that. It's not his fault he doesn't believe in ghosts. I guess it has a lot to do with the way people are raised or something ..."

"I blame society," Marilyn added plainly. "And bad television programming. And sometimes I blame gummy bears. All squishy candies, actually, but that's a long story."

"Alright, Auntie," Kathy said, waving her arms around wildly. "He's coming!"

And as Harold Chavez approached them, he slowed his pace and smiled an awkward smile. "Hello, girls. How are you?"

Alicia waved at her father nervously. "Hi, Dad! How was work today?"

"Yeah," Kathy said with a friendly, unsuspicious smile. "Tell us about work, Mr. Chavez."

Alicia's dad hesitated before speaking. He stopped right in front of them and wanted to, but couldn't, reach past them for the door handle. They were blocking his way into the house. And although he couldn't see her, Marilyn was standing right behind them, directly in front of the door. "Uh ... why would you two girls want to hear about work? That's boring grown-up stuff."

Kathy had to think of something quick to say. "Work sounds interesting! I want to work someday. And I want to work on interesting things ... like, maybe ... movies."

Alicia's dad lifted an eyebrow at her, and Marilyn whispered something into Kathy's ear.

Kathy smiled uncomfortably. "Science fiction movies are my favorite. If I was an adult, I'd probably like to watch old science fiction movies at work."

"Kathy!" hissed Alicia.

Marilyn covered her mouth as she began to giggle.

Alicia's dad took a step backward and looked at the two girls. "Kathy," he began slowly, "I'm sure you are aware that work involves a lot more than watching old movies. In fact, most adults don't watch old movies at work—"

"But you do!" she dared to say.

At that point, Alicia cleared her throat. "Kathy's dad told her a little bit about the films you're working on, Dad, and she's just curious about—"

"Oh yes!" he exclaimed. He then nodded enthusiastically, a little too enthusiastically. "Of course she's curious! And I have almost finished repairing and restoring those amazing films. What an interesting experience it has been to work on those ... delightful films."

Marilyn eyed him carefully. "He looks like he's hiding something."

Alicia's dad reached out for the front door again, but the girls wouldn't budge. "Now I am extremely hungry and would like to get inside the house now, if you don't mind, girls."

Reluctantly, Kathy and Alicia moved aside, as did Marilyn.

Kathy had to think fast. "Will you be going to our school's movie night this Friday, Mr. Chavez?"

Alicia's dad froze in place. "Ah ... no. I won't be going," he answered with an odd look on his face. "Excuse me. Very hungry now."

"But why not?" Kathy continued, desperate to find out anything she could.

"Well," Alicia's dad looked around nervously as he reached forward to grasp the door handle. He pushed the door open. "I can't be there. I-I just can't. There are lots of reasons why. Grown-up reasons, and I hope we're having Italian food tonight! Ummmmm. Yummy stuff that Italian food!"

And with that, Harold Chavez slipped inside

the house and, with an awfully panicked look on his face, closed the door behind him.

"Italian food?" Alicia asked herself out loud.

"Garlic," Kathy replied. "There's lots of garlic in Italian food, Ally. Obviously, your father is afraid of vampires."

"I can't believe this is happening. My life is over. My dad is going crazy because of vampires and old movies. I don't get it. I know there's a connection. There has to be. But what is it?"

Kathy rubbed her hands together in deep thought. She knew there was something going on—something sinister. Something unnatural. And she also knew that she and Alicia would have to be the ones to put a stop to it. "The movies your dad is working on has to have something to do with those vampires. I know it."

Alicia rolled her eyes in frustration. "So we know he's working on old movies ... and that one of them is probably Condemned Vampire Cookout."

"Yes, Ally," Kathy replied. "But there's something else going on here, something more serious. You were right about your dad. He *is* acting different. But working on some cheesy science fiction movie shouldn't do that to him."

Marilyn reminded her, "You said something

interesting about the boy, the one listening in on your conversation today."

"Yes," Alicia answered. "He said that it was interesting that my dad was working on old movies at work, and then he said it was also interesting that they are showing an old movie on Friday at the drive-in."

"I think you girls need to talk to that boy," Marilyn suggested with a sly smile.

"Ewww," Alicia said. "He was strange."

"And he was cute," Kathy smiled. "I volunteer to have a talk with him ... for the good of the planet, I mean."

"That is so gross," Alicia said with a smirk on her face.

"If I have to talk to a cute, dark-haired boy with deep brown eyes and amazing style to help save the world, then I will."

"We don't have a lot of time, Kathy," Marilyn reminded her. "According to The Order's latest update, we now know that the space vampires have threatened to end the world on Friday, which also happens to be movie night. There's an emergency council meeting in about an hour. If I get any new information, I'll let you know. If that boy knows anything, you must let me know as soon as possible."

"I will, Auntie," was Kathy's response.

Alicia sighed. "I think school is going to be very interesting tomorrow."

# Chapter 8

The school hallways were a mess, filled with students, chatter, and busy teachers. It certainly wasn't the place for any serious sort of conversation. Especially in between classes. But as soon as Kathy saw what she thought might be the back of Alicia's jacket, she rushed over to her through the crowd and tapped her on the shoulder.

"Hey, Ally!"

"Hi!" Alicia turned to acknowledge her, but there were too many other students around, pushing and shoving their way past them. "Hey, Kathy! I'm stuck!"

"I can't find that kid anywhere! I even asked some of those guys who always have detention ... nobody knows who he is!"

"This is not good news!"

Kathy tried, but just couldn't keep her place next to Alicia. Within seconds of standing there, a tall boy in a basketball jersey elbowed her in the arm, hopefully by accident, and another kid stomped on her foot. It was almost time for the tardy bell to ring, and students had changed; they had gone into survival mode — they were only looking out for themselves. "Meet me in the library!" Kathy called back as a wave of students began to push her down the hallway. "Get a pass from your teacher! I'll be there after the bell rings!"

Alicia couldn't hold her ground any longer. She stood on the toes of her shoes to watch as Kathy was being dragged farther away from her. "Okay! I'll try!"

The school library

"I don't think he's a student here."

Alicia crossed her arms. "Then why was he here yesterday?"

"He was watching football practice ... *after* school. That doesn't mean he's a student here," Kathy said in her quiet library voice. "And I looked for him in the halls, I described him to other kids. Nobody's ever heard of him or seen him around before."

"But you don't even know his name," Alicia reminded her. "You can't just go around describing him to people. Maybe they haven't seen him yet. Maybe he's new."

"If he was new, he'd stick out even more. So why hasn't anybody seen him today?"

Alicia looked to the ceiling, contemplating Kathy's question. "Maybe he's absent."

"Hmmm."

"Or maybe you're just not very good at describing people," Alicia suggested.

"Look, we don't have a lot of time, Ally. We've got to find this kid and figure out what he knows." Kathy lowered her head and swiftly glanced around the library. "I asked Mr. Walsh to meet us here. He should be here any minute."

"Doesn't he have a class to teach?"

"Ally," Kathy growled. "We're trying to save the world!"

Alicia shook her head and then noticed Mr. Walsh rushing through the library. She raised her hand into the air to get his attention.

"Perfect. He's here."

Alicia didn't seem very interested. "Did you pick out an outfit for movie night?"

Kathy's face lit up. "Yes! Oh my gosh. Wait until you see it. I ordered the skirt the other day online, but I already had the shirt and stuff. It's so retro."

"I wish I could order clothes online," Alicia mumbled.

"So you're going, right? You don't have to wear something retro."

Alicia frowned. "I don't really want to go, but since it sounds like I have to …"

"Girls!" Mr. Walsh interrupted, out of breath. "I don't have a lot of time. I have a student watching my class, but the other students could still start a fire or break the windows and escape."

Kathy pulled out the chair next to her. "Take a seat. We'll be as quick as we can be. But this is official business."

"What's going on?" he asked them as he sat down.

Alicia leaned in to say, "We're looking for a boy."

Mr. Walsh adjusted his glasses. "Okay. I don't think that's any of my business."

Kathy frowned at him. "We think he knows something about …" she paused to scan their surroundings, "… the space vampires."

Alicia added, "We don't have a lot of time to explain. The boy has dark hair and dark eyes."

"He wears cool clothes … like he might be in a

band or something."

"No," Alicia disagreed. "He doesn't look *that* cool."

"Yes he does."

Alicia thought about it. "I guess he dresses alright. Sort of. But his hair is messy."

"In a good way."

Alicia then raised a finger into the air and said, "Oh! And he's very pale."

Mr. Walsh tilted his head. "Pale?"

"Yes, pale," Kathy agreed with a quick nod.

Mr. Walsh asked, "Pale, messy hair, looks like he's in a band ... and he's a student here?"

Kathy tapped her fingers on the table. "That's the part we're not too sure about yet."

"Hmmm." Mr. Walsh said as he stared through Alicia, going over the description of the mysterious boy again in his head. "Is he tall or short?"

"Hard to say," Kathy answered in all seriousness. "We've only seen him while he was sitting."

"Ah."

Alicia suddenly sat straight up. "Oh! He likes bubble gum!"

Kathy quickly nodded in agreement. "Yes! He does!"

Mr. Walsh squinted his eyes at something behind the two girls. He then lowered his head and, as discreetly as possible, pointed a finger across the table. "Is that him?"

Both girls slowly turned around to see a boy—the exact one they had just been describing—blow an extra-large pink bubble. He was standing at the entrance of the library, leaning against the door, staring right at them with those dark, piercing eyes.

Kathy carefully reached into the front pocket of her backpack and pulled out a small round mirror, she peered into it nervously to check for any sort of shininess on her face. "Yeah, that's him."

Mr. Walsh stood and straightened his vest. "I have to get back to class, girls. Let me know what's going on as soon as you can."

Both girls nodded in response and then watched as Mr. Walsh took cautious steps toward the library's entrance. He did what he could to walk past the boy without seeming too obvious that they had just been talking about him. But of course, this didn't look very natural as Mr. Walsh wasn't a very good actor.

Kathy, looking more unsure of herself than usual, snatched up her backpack and rose from her seat. She motioned for Alicia to follow her lead. "He knows we want to talk to him. So let's just go over there and get this over with."

Alicia hardened her stare on the boy. "I'm ready," she lied.

The two girls, not really sure what they were about to get themselves into, walked across the library and over to where the boy was standing. As they approached, he smiled confidently.

Kathy took the lead. "Hi."

"Hello," the boy said in return. He was wearing a dark-gray T-shirt with a band on it whose members appeared to be made up of werewolves and mummies.

"Remember us from yesterday? At the football practice?" Kathy asked.

"Yes."

"My name's Kathy Preston. And this is my friend Alicia Chavez."

The boy's eyes went to the floor. "Nice to meet you. My name's Kevan."

"We don't have a lot of time to explain, Kevan," Kathy continued. "But we'd really like to talk to you about something."

"Yeah," Alicia said. "We've been looking for you all morning."

"I've been looking for you, too," Kevan answered.

"What for?" Kathy asked.

"Same reason ... to talk."

Alicia stepped forward. "What we want to talk about is serious business. And it involves my dad."

"I know," Kevan answered.

Kathy and Alicia immediately looked at each other in surprise. Kathy placed a hand on her hip and studied Kevan's face. "What do you mean, *you know*?"

Kevan reached into his pocket and pulled out a wadded up gum wrapper. He looked at both girls, and the confused looks on their faces, as he opened the wrapper and put it to his mouth. After spitting his gum into the paper, he smiled wide.

Kathy and Alicia gasped.

Kevan's bright white fangs gleamed vibrantly even under the cheap fluorescent lights of the Sinatra Middle School Library. His eyes shifted about the room before he leaned in to say, "I think we can help each other out."

# Chapter 9

Kevan quickened his pace down the hallway as both girls followed close behind.

"Where's he taking us?" Alicia was extremely worried and her voice wobbled. "We can't leave the school. We'll get in trouble!"

"We're not leaving the school," Kevan said to them. "What I need to show you is here. *Inside* the school ... in the theater arts storage room."

Alicia grabbed onto the back of Kathy's shoulder to whisper, "This is crazy!"

Kevan stopped, spinning around to face them, his piercing eyes now intimidating, even a bit commanding. "Why is it crazy? Because I'm a vampire?"

The girls looked at him with blank eyes, surprised at the bluntness of the question. "Um, sort of," Alicia answered with not only her voice shaking, but her knees as well.

"When I show you what they're keeping here at

your school, maybe you'll trust me," Kevan replied. "Of course, I don't expect you to trust me *now*, but you will soon."

Kathy studied him closely, and as she did, her face changed. She suddenly realized something that she'd missed before and just couldn't keep it to herself. Of course, you know by now that Kathy had a hard time keeping anything to herself, which in some cases is good and in some bad … but in this case, a case in which one is dealing with a vampire, there aren't really any set rules. "How are you able to withstand sunlight, huh?!"

Kevan's eyes widened. "Your sun has no effect on me."

"My sun?" Kathy asked. "What are you talking about?"

"I don't have time to explain," he said to them. "Please help me find the theater arts storage room. Are we headed the right way?"

Alicia put on a brave face. "Why should we trust you?"

Kevan hesitated and his face grew serious, almost sad. "Because I don't want your planet destroyed. That's why."

Kathy glanced at Alicia with a look of uncertainty on her face. "You're a space vampire, aren't you?"

Kevan rolled his eyes. "If that's what you want to call it. I can explain later. But for now, we need to hurry. We have to stop them before tomorrow."

"Stop who?" Kathy asked, even though she was quite certain she knew what the answer would be.

"The other vampires," Kevan answered. "They want to change everything on your planet. And if that doesn't work … they'll probably try to destroy it."

"But why?" Alicia asked desperately.

"Because they feel insulted. It's a pride thing. Your planet hurt their feelings. I don't know how to explain it all right now. We just have to hurry."

Kathy's face hardened. "All right. Let's go find that storage room." She formed her hand into a tight fist and held it out in front of Kevan's face. "But if you turn on us … you'll regret it."

Alicia nodded frantically. "Yeah! And I've got some garlic in my pockets!"

Kathy turned to her, knowing that Alicia could not have known to put garlic in her pockets that morning, and then looked back at Kevan to see his reaction.

Kevan only smiled. "Sorry. Garlic doesn't work on me."

"Well," Kathy replied, trying to mask the fear in her voice, "a punch in the stomach will work on anyone. So watch it!"

"No problem," Kevan agreed. "I've heard the blood on your planet tastes funny anyway."

As the three of them stood in silence in front of the storage room, Kathy slowly reached out for the door handle before she turned to face Kevan. "It's probably locked. You probably didn't think about that, did you?"

Kevan reached into his jeans' pocket and pulled out a shiny silver key. "Actually, I did."

Alicia's face lit up. "How did you get that?"

"My uncle had a copy of the key … until I took it."

The girls moved aside so Kevan could open the door for them.

"Explain further," Kathy insisted.

"Well," he began, "my uncle, Sir Vilester Ghoulingheart, provided the movie for your school's movie night. So the school said they'd store the film here to keep it safe. He told the school that he wanted a copy of the key because the film was important to him. He said the film was a rare piece of Hollywood history."

"The film is in this storage room?"

"It's supposed to be," Kevan answered. "It should have been delivered today by some guy my uncle hired to—"

At that exact moment, a noise startled them.

Alicia latched onto Kathy's arm and squeezed tightly. "Someone's coming!"

Kathy looked all around in a panic. The hallway leading to the storage closet was a dead end, and the three of them were standing at the dead end of it. Kevan quickly unlocked the door and pushed it open. Inside the room was nothing but darkness, and the sound of footsteps was getting closer.

"We'll have to hide inside," Kathy suggested.

"But ... it's dark!" Alicia complained. "And ... and he's a vampire! I don't think you're supposed to hang out in the dark with vampires!"

"I know, Ally!" Kathy didn't know what else they could do. "He's not going to bite us. Right, Kevan?"

"Of course not. Don't worry. I've already had my lunch."

Alicia looked at Kathy with the most intense fear in her eyes. And she looked a little queasy, too.

"Quick! Come on!" Kevan said. "I can see in the dark! Follow me. We can hide behind one of those big boxes in the back!"

Kathy and Alicia had to take his word for it.

Whoever was coming down the hall towards them was getting closer. And if Kathy and Alicia wanted a shot at saving the world from whatever was going to happen to it on Friday, listening to a teenaged vampire named Kevan might be their only chance. So they each grabbed onto one of Kevan's cold, icy arms and allowed him to lead them into the back of the storage room.

"It smells weird in here," Alicia griped.

"Shhhh!"

The footsteps stopped at the storage room's entrance.

"Hmmm," a woman's voice said. "The door's already open."

Then a man's voice said, "Maybe they were expecting us." And the man's voice sounded very familiar — especially to Alicia.

"You can place the film in here," the woman said, "… if I can find the light switch."

Alicia, afraid that she might be seen when the lights were on, carefully pushed herself in further behind the boxes. The three of them listened as the woman patted her hand against the wall. Alicia barely pulled her arm out of sight as the light switch clicked. She looked next to her, hoping that it was Kathy that she was leaned up against in the small space they were crammed into, but it wasn't.

A smile with a pair of gleaming white fangs greeted her instead. She gasped, covered her mouth, and then saw Kathy on the other side of Kevan with a finger placed across her lips, begging with frantic eyes for Alicia to remain quiet.

"Ah, yes," the woman continued, "there are plenty of shelves in here. You can set them down anywhere you'd like, Mr. Chavez."

Kathy's mouth dropped open.

"Hmmm," Mr. Chavez replied. "Actually, I'd feel much more comfortable leaving the film inside a safe."

Kathy carefully eyed the boxes in front of them, looking for a spot to peek out through. She just had to get a glimpse of Alicia's dad.

"A safe?" the woman asked.

"Yes, Mrs. Shelton," Mr. Chavez answered in a calm voice. "My client and I would like to do everything we can to protect this precious piece of art."

Alicia's eyes looked like they might pop out of their sockets.

"But we don't have a safe in the theater arts storage room ... or in any room in the school that I'm aware of, Mr. Chavez."

"Well, that might be a problem."

"Mr. Chavez," Mrs. Shelton began, "the room will be locked. No one except me, the custodial staff, and your gracious client will have a key."

Kathy, now on her tiptoes, found a spot in between a few boxes to spy through. She could see Alicia's father's arms, clutching four round metal canisters to his chest.

"The film will be perfectly safe," Mrs. Shelton tried to assure him. "Are there people interested in stealing it?"

"It has an interesting history." Mr. Chavez then hugged the film canisters even tighter. "Hollywood stuff. It's a rare film. It hasn't been seen anywhere. Ever. Digitally restored and then placed back onto film reels with a foreign technology that even I don't understand completely. Our client wishes to keep the viewing as traditional as possible. The students at this school and their families will be very lucky to see it."

Kathy glanced at Alicia, and Alicia appeared to be in shock.

Mr. Chavez then set the film down on a shelf near the door and motioned for Mrs. Shelton to exit the room first. Kathy watched as Mr. Chavez reached for the light switch, but stopped himself. He took one last glance at the film canisters ... one long, curious look, and then turned out the light and closed the door behind him.

Kathy, Alicia, and Kevan remained still as they listened to a key being placed into the door's lock, and then a sharp click sound afterward. And when the sound of footsteps began to disappear down the hallway, Alicia pulled out her cell phone, activated the screen for some light, and then sighed. "What's going on with my dad?"

Kathy activated the screen of her phone also, and shined it on Kevan's pale, smooth face. "You seem to know a lot about this whole situation."

Kevan, unable to look Alicia in the eye, frowned and shook his head. "I've heard your dad's name mentioned a few times. He's working for my Uncle Vilester."

# Chapter 10

Later that evening.

Alicia stared across the dinner table at her father, looking for any signs of strange behavior. He was chewing his food extra slow, and his eyes were unfocused. Alicia couldn't figure out what her father was or wasn't looking at, because he didn't actually seem to be looking at anything at all.

"Dad?" she said. And when her father didn't answer, her mother and her little brother Jimmy looked at Mr. Chavez expectantly.

"Harold?" her mother tried. "Ally is talking to you."

But Mr. Chavez stared off into space and still said nothing.

"Daddy looks like a coo coo bird," Jimmy announced. "Why is he so crazy now?"

Their mother shot a warning glance at Jimmy.

Even if you are only six years old, calling your father crazy is still a rude thing to do. "Your father is not crazy. He's tired. He's worked a long week." And even though she had said it herself, she didn't truly seem to believe it, because, in reality, he did seem a bit crazy. There was worry in her eyes. "He just finished an important project. Haven't you, Harold?"

Mr. Chavez suddenly shook as if a jolt of electricity went through his body. "What, dear?"

"Work," his wife reminded him. "It's made you tired, hasn't it, Harold?"

"Yes!" he answered with an overly enthusiastic smile. "It sure has been draining the life out of me!"

Alicia squirmed as she thought about the words her father had used. "Dad?" she asked softly.

Her father looked at her. "Yes, Ally?"

"Since the project is over, you're going to start catching up on some sleep and try to relax now, right?"

Her father let out a boisterous, hearty laugh and slammed his fist on the table.

"Harold!" her mother cried out in surprise.

"Relaxation!" he said in between a few chuckles. "Yes! And I took tomorrow off, also!"

Jimmy scrunched up his face. "Coo coo bird."

"That's great, Dad." Alicia wanted to be encouraging, and hoped that her father really did want to relax now that the project was over with, but she didn't trust something about the way he was acting. She could still hear his voice in her head, talking to the theater arts teacher, Mrs. Shelton. She wanted to believe that he didn't know anything about the space vampires, that Kevan was wrong, that her father just couldn't be connected to them in any way. But she had to be sure. "And after you relax here at home for the day, maybe you can relax with the whole family at the drive-in."

Mr. Chavez recoiled in his seat. "NEVER!" he yelled in complete terror.

All eyes went wide as they stared at Mr. Chavez in complete silence.

Alicia cleared her throat. "Ooooooookay. I was just making a suggestion."

Alicia's mother reached out for her husband's hand. "What's going on with you, Harold?"

Mr. Chavez was trembling, crumpled over in his chair, and looked like he was about to jump through the dining room window for an escape. "I-I just don't want to go to movie night. That's all. No one can force me to go. Not even you, Tina!"

"*Force* you?" his wife replied in confusion.

Alicia quickly thought of something to ask her father before it was too late. "Is it because it's a vampire movie?"

"Who told you that?!" he snapped.

"The school, Dad." Alicia was frightened. The panicked look on her father's face was difficult to stomach. "They said the movie's called Condemned Vampire Cookout."

Her father's left eye began to twitch. "Oh, did they? Huh. That's interesting. What a title. Sounds like a terrible movie. Just not my type of thing. And I don't approve of this family attending a movie with a title like that."

"WHAT?!" Jimmy yelled. "I'm going to see those vampires, mister!"

"Oh no you aren't, Jimmy!"

"Harold!" Tina snapped. "Jimmy has been looking forward to seeing that movie all week. It's approved for all ages."

"That doesn't mean I approve, Tina!"

"It sounds good to me!" Jimmy said defensively. "I tried to look it up on the Internet, but I couldn't find it on there."

Mr. Chavez shot a look at his wife. "Since when does he use the Internet? He's only six years old!"

"He looked it up on my phone, Dad," Alicia explained.

Mr. Chavez leaned in toward his son and looked at him with a soft, doe-eyed gaze. "You wouldn't like the film anyway, Jimmy. It's old, and it's in black-and-white."

Alicia gasped—quietly though since she was doing her best to hide it—because she knew at that moment that her father had, in fact, seen the film in one way or another. No one had said anything about it being in black-and-white. Confirmed—Condemned Vampire Cookout was something Harold Chavez knew something about. Something more than he was admitting to.

"Oh, he doesn't care if it's in black-and-white, Harold," her mother told him.

"How'd you know that, Dad?" Alicia asked.

The twitch returned to Mr. Chavez's eye. "How'd I know *what*, ... Daughter?"

"That it was in black and white."

He smiled awkwardly and thought about the question for a moment only to answer in the simplest way, "I don't know."

Alicia slowly nodded. "I'm not hungry right now, Mom. Can I finish later?"

"Yes, of course," her mother answered in a kind, distant voice.

Mr. Chavez had his eyes locked onto Alicia's. They were cold and menacing and there was something very different about them. They weren't anything like her father's eyes at all—and at that moment, he was a complete stranger to her.

And as Alicia got up from her seat, he didn't break that horrible stare until she turned away from the table to rush up to her room in a panic. She needed to call Kathy for an update. With the new information they had learned about Kevan's Uncle Ghoulingheart, Marilyn was supposed to be doing a background investigation on the name. And if Kathy didn't have any new information to share with her, she knew that she was probably going to go into a complete panic. Alicia had no idea what to do next—her father was certainly losing his mind.

At the table, Jimmy was using his fork to crush several peas into a mushy green mess. He had a pretty serious scowl on his face, too. "Someone better take me to see that vampire movie tomorrow, or I'm gonna LOSE IT!"

"Jimmy!" his mother hissed.

# Chapter 11

Friday Morning.

As soon as Alicia spotted Kathy in the school courtyard, she rushed up to her, pushing through several students along the way. Tired, groggy, and sloppily dressed, Alicia was at her wits end with the entire situation. She had confirmed that her father was becoming a complete nutcase. And it was also quite possible that he was in cahoots with vampires from another planet. This was not an easy thing for a teenaged girl to digest—at least not for a girl like Alicia.

"Listen," Kathy began in all seriousness, "whatever's going on, we have to stay calm and be cool about it."

"That's going to be a little difficult," Alicia replied with an intense look in her eyes. "If you'd found out your dad was working for vampires, you'd be freaking out, too!"

"Shhhh," Kathy warned. "My dad is the one running the show over there, remember? That 'client' contacted him first."

Alicia relaxed a little as she thought about it. "True."

"I'm just as concerned about all of this as you are."

Alicia nodded.

"Okay then. Look, I don't know what's going on here, but we've got to find that kid Kevan." Kathy looked around anxiously.

"Why?" To Alicia, it all felt hopeless. It was already Friday. She was certain that the wheels of doom were already in motion. The horrible Earth-ending thing that was about to happen, was going to happen no matter what a couple of eighth-grade girls did to try and stop it.

"Like I told you last night on the phone, Marilyn wants to meet Kevan. She wants to talk to him," Kathy explained. There was something sparkly in her eyes, something hopeful — she still believed that the world could be saved. "Marilyn talked to Mr. Walsh last night. He's supposed to be checking the school's records. He's going to help find out what classes Kevan's in so we can all talk."

Just then, Mr. Walsh tapped Alicia on the shoulder. "He's not a student here."

Kathy let out a strained breath and placed a hand on her forehead. "I don't know what to do. Marilyn's going to be here any minute. I told her we'd find him."

"Let's get back to my classroom and wait there until she arrives," Mr. Walsh suggested.

Alicia checked the time on her phone. "School starts in about fifteen minutes."

"Let's hurry," Kathy urged them.

Mr. Walsh's classroom always seemed a bit cold, which was fine and much appreciated by everyone in the humid fall—but in winter, it seemed that only Mr. Walsh enjoyed it.

"Mr. Walsh," Kathy said with her arms wrapped tightly around her, "it's like an icebox in here."

Alicia, seated in a chair in front of Mr. Walsh's desk, looked over at Kathy in agreement. She was shivering.

"It'll warm up around noon," he answered with a smile.

Then suddenly, the sound of electrical fizzing and crackling overtook the air around them. The lights flickered and there seemed to be a strange but recognizable smell ... and for some reason, the smell was a lot like burning caramel. Alicia hunched down in her seat and covered her face with her hands as Mr. Walsh backed away from his desk, his eyes darting everywhere.

Kathy smiled. "It's Marilyn." She then scooted her chair over and reached behind her, grabbing a hold of another chair and dragging it into a spot between herself and a very frightened Alicia. She patted on the seat of the chair with confidence.

And with one loud pop—a sound so strange that it almost sounded as if it was happening in reverse—Marilyn appeared in the chair Kathy had just prepared for her.

Alicia let out a shaky breath. "Hi," she squeaked.

Marilyn smiled. "Hello, dear."

Mr. Walsh, pretending this time that he wasn't startled or taken aback by the small electrical storm that had just occurred inside his classroom, took to his seat again. "How's it going, Marilyn?"

"Not so great, Johnathan," Marilyn answered. She turned to Kathy. "I found out a lot of information about this Sir Ghoulingheart. And not a single bit of it is good."

"Oh no," Alicia said, her lips trembling.

Marilyn turned to Alicia with a nurturing look in her eyes. "And I'm afraid that there really is a connection with him and your father, Ally."

Now very interested, Mr. Walsh leaned forward. "What did you find out?"

Marilyn looked at all three of them, hoping that they were prepared to hear what she was about to explain. "Sir Ghoulingheart is an original member of a popular car club that consists of vampires from all over the universe. And probably other universes as well."

Kathy smirked. "A car club?"

"Other universes?" asked Mr. Walsh.

"Yes. I know it sounds strange, but it's true. Coolness exists all over the universe, and others. Not just on Earth."

Alicia had a very good question. "What does any of this have to do with my dad?"

Marilyn frowned. "Well, that's why I'd really like to speak with your friend Kevan."

"He's not our friend," Alicia replied. "He's a vampire."

"It's not his fault he's a vampire," Kathy added.

Alicia's mouth dropped open. "Ewww, Kathy! You like him, don't you?"

"No way. I was just saying—"

"Girls!" Marilyn cried out. "We have bigger

issues going on here! Let's focus."

"Sorry," both girls said in unison.

Marilyn composed herself. "Now, where is this boy Kevan?"

"That's the problem," Mr. Walsh said. "We don't know."

"All right," Marilyn got up from her seat and brushed something from the sleeves of her sweater. Soft little dust clouds formed around her face and then gently spread out all around her. Both girls scooted their chairs away and covered their faces as Marilyn began to cough. Mr. Walsh let out a quick sneeze. "A little sand from Egypt," she said. "Sorry."

She then closed her eyes and lifted her head toward the ceiling, and said in all seriousness, "I know a way to locate any vampire within a three mile radius."

Kathy gleamed with excitement. "You do?!"

"Yes, of course, dear," Marilyn answered, her eyes still closed. "I work with quite an assortment of ghosts, goblins, and ghouls for a living. I've learned a few tricks along the way."

Kathy could hardly contain her excitement, but Alicia ... well, she was just doing her best not to jump out of her seat and run for the door. She studied Kathy's aunt with great concern, hoping that whatever she was about to do would go smoothly and not accidentally conjure up some other vampire that might be lurking in the area. Now that she knew they existed, she wasn't very interested in meeting any more of them.

Marilyn raised her arms out to her sides and let out a long breath. "Vampires near, vampires far ... come out Kevan Ghoulingheart, wherever you are!"

And for a few seconds, the room was silent.

"That's it?" Kathy asked.

"Well, yes," Marilyn said with a simple shrug. "What did you expect?"

A light knock at the door surprised all of them. Alicia gasped, Mr. Walsh scooted back in his chair, and Kathy grabbed a hold of Marilyn's half-solid arm.

"It's him," Marilyn announced.

"Him who?" Alicia asked.

"Kevan."

Mr. Walsh slowly stood, straightened his tie, and then looked over his glasses at the door. "Uh ... come in."

The door opened and in walked Kevan. He was in the middle of blowing a very large pink bubble. After it popped, he looked at Kathy and Alicia. "Maybe I should give you girls my phone number so you can text me when you need something. That spell-thing you guys used kinda stung a little."

Kathy quickly let go of Marilyn's arm and ran her fingers through her dark bangs. "Oh. Okay. That would be nice."

Alicia giggled.

Marilyn stepped forward and held out her hand to Kevan, inviting him to shake it. "My name is Marilyn Preston. I represent The Mystical Order of Ghosts, Enigmas, and Cryptids on behalf of the planet Earth."

Kevan lowered his head to the ground. "Are you going to arrest me or something?"

"No," Marilyn answered, surprised by the question. "We don't arrest people. I just want to ask you a few questions about your uncle, Sir Vilester Ghoulingheart."

Kevan shut the door behind him and then looked at each of them with sad eyes. "He hasn't told me what's going on. I don't think he trusts me."

"And I think I know why," Marilyn replied.

Kevan looked at her with uncertainty. "Really?"

"Yes, Kevan." She answered gently. "I know he expects you to follow in his footsteps ... to be a great vampire leader, doesn't he?"

"Yes."

"And it's not what you want to do."

"How'd you know that?" Kevan asked.

"Because The Order showed me your application, Kevan. You applied to join your planet's chapter last year."

Kevan's eyes instantly went glassy. He wanted to look away, to hide his face from all of them.

"I know you're different from the rest of your family, Kevan. I know you want to help others."

"But my application was rejected."

"No, it wasn't," Marilyn clarified. "Your father and uncle intervened."

Kevan's eyes widened. "What do you mean?"

"They were against us contacting you for an interview, and because you are still considered a teenager on your planet, we had to get their permission first. I know this because The Order told me. They allowed me to review the application."

Kevan's face turned angry and his eyes piercing. "You see?! This is why I don't want anything to do with them! My father especially! He goes along with anything my uncle says!"

Kathy and Alicia glanced back at Mr. Walsh. They didn't know what to say or do. Kevan was obviously upset and hurting. Mr. Walsh nodded and held his hand out in front of him, signaling for the girls to allow Marilyn to handle it.

"Kevan," Marilyn continued, "I think your father and your uncle mean well."

Kevan now looked furious. "How can you say that?! They want to destroy your planet!"

"But Kevan—"

"And you know what else?!" Kevan asked. "They want me to work on cars with them! Cars they collect from all kinds of planets like yours! I don't want to build hot rods! I want to do what *I* want to do! I want to learn the guitar and play in a band!"

Marilyn approached him. She placed a hand on his shoulder. "I understand."

Kevan looked up into her caring eyes. "I don't even want to be a vampire anymore."

"Oh no, Kevan," she said with such kindness, a kindness that seemed very foreign to Kevan. "You can't give up who you are. I know you feel different from the rest of your family, but you can't change the very thing that makes you special. It's more important than anything in the universe that you just be you. Understand?"

Kevan looked over at Alicia and Kathy before turning his focus back to Marilyn. On his face was determination and strength. "Whatever info you need on my uncle, I'll do what I can to help. My dad's just going along with it, but I don't think he's behind any of it. My uncle's the leader."

"Thank you, Kevan. And I promise to put in a good word for you with The Order so that when you are allowed to join us, you can."

Mr. Walsh cleared his throat. "Sorry to interrupt, but the bell's about to ring. Students will be flooding into my classroom any minute."

"He's right," Alicia confirmed. "We have to get out of here."

"How about the theater arts storage room?" Kevan suggested. "We have to get that film out of there and hide it before tonight."

"Why?" Marilyn asked.

"Because when Alicia's dad put it into digital format, they were able to add in secret messages — messages to brainwash the world ... one student at a time."

# CHapter 12

Floating miles above Earth in a darkened garage, hidden away in the lower parts of an enormous silver disk-shaped spaceship, Sir Vilester Ghoulingheart and his brother Shawn tinkered and tankered with something referred to as a carburetor. These carburetor things were used, at one time or another, in cars on several planets in several galaxies and had something to do with how fuel was used in older car engines. And old cars and older car engines were of great interest to the Ghoulingheart brothers — when they weren't thinking about changing the future of Earth, that is.

"Shawn," Vilester said in his deep raspy voice. His shiny black hair was perfectly slicked back, his widow's peak extra widowy.

"Yes, Vile?" his brother Shawn asked. He had one of his claw-like hands around a wrench, the other holding a screwdriver. And as Shawn waited for his brother's response, he nervously wiped the side of his chin against the greasy white T-shirt he was wearing under a pair of dark-blue overalls.

Vilester stepped away from the metal table they were working at and stared at his brother with beady red eyes. "Where's that boy of yours?" he asked coldly.

Shawn tilted his head, puzzled. "I'm not too sure."

"Is that so?" Vilester questioned further.

And since Shawn had always been intimidated by his older brother's boney, hunched-over, scraggly appearance—even though the two of them looked remarkably similar—all he could think of to do was smile at him in return.

"He should be here with us, learning about cars," Vilester hissed. He looked down over his pointy nose at his brother Shawn. "Don't you agree?"

"Yes, Vile. I agree."

Vilester eyed him intensely. "Then why isn't he here?"

Shawn put down his wrench and screwdriver, then nervously wiped his hands on his overalls and sighed. "Vile, you know he's not particularly interested in cars."

"I am well aware," Vilester replied with an upturned nose. "But where does your son go while we work so hard on these cars? We have so much to prepare for, brother. Tonight is a very important night. And Kevan has done absolutely nothing to assist us in our preparations. All he does is disappear whenever we need him around." Vilester scratched at his sharp, prominent chin in disappointment.

Shawn wanted to answer his brother, but didn't wish to upset him. So he went about it with care. "Kevan has been out exploring."

"Exploring what?"

"The city."

"Looking for what?"

"Other kids his age, I think."

Vilester gasped in horror, clutching at his sunken chest. "Earth kids?!"

Shawn seemed surprised by his brother's reaction. "Yes. There are no other sorts of children there, I believe."

Vilester contorted his thin face into the most intimidating look that he could create with it and leaned in closer to his brother. "You are his father. And it is your responsibility to keep him in line. Running around with Earth children isn't healthy for him."

Shawn suddenly looked frightened. "Do they have cooties?"

Vilester raised his arched eyebrows and rolled his eyes. "They have poisonous ideas about things … About us!"

Shawn nodded in agreement. "Yes, of course."

"So instead of hanging around a bunch of misguided Earth brats, Kevan should be here with his father and his uncle. He should be helping to prepare for tonight's event."

"You are right, dear brother."

Sir Vilester Ghoulingheart smiled a most chilling and wicked grin, displaying the whitest, sharpest fangs. "Tonight will change our existence. After we alter things on Earth, we will be hailed as heroes by vampires everywhere!"

Shawn could see the determination and the confidence in his brother's eyes. And he could certainly feel the power in his frightening voice.

"Movie night with Earth's Sinatra Middle School will be unforgettable … for *us*!" Vilester let out a sinister laugh that roared and echoed throughout the spaceship's entire garage. And it most definitely made the nickname Vile seem most appropriate.

# Chapter 13

"Why didn't you just take the film from the storage room when we were there the first time?!" Kathy asked Kevan impatiently. They were walking as quickly as they possibly could toward the theater arts hallway.

"Because I didn't have anything to replace it with. I have another film with me this time to leave in its place."

Just then, Alicia stopped dead in her tracks, holding her phone close to her face. "I just got a text from my brother."

Kathy spun around. "From *Jimmy*?"

"Yes."

"Jimmy's only six. How'd he get a cell phone?"

"He didn't," Alicia answered dryly. "He used my dad's phone. My dad's off from work today. He's supposed to be resting. But—"

"Come on!" Kevan called back. He was several

feet ahead of them with Marilyn. "We don't have a lot of time!"

Kathy ignored him. She could tell from the look on Alicia's face that something serious was happening. "Isn't Jimmy supposed to be in school?"

"Yes."

"What does the text say?"

"It says, 'Dad use computer to look for spaceships. Then he hide under blanket now. I took phone.'"

Kathy felt a tingling sensation ripple through her from head to toe. "Wait. *What*?" was all she could think of to say.

"I think my dad's on the Internet," Alicia realized. "I think that's what Jimmy's trying to say."

Kathy moved in closer to get a better look at the screen of Alicia's phone. "Ask Jimmy where he is. Ask him what website your dad was on. Oh, and ask him—"

"Okay, okay. Hold on," Alicia said as she quickly worked her fingers to type a message to her brother.

"Come on, girls!" Marilyn's voice carried down the hallway.

Kathy turned to see that Kevan and Marilyn

were very eager to get to the storage room, but she didn't have time to explain to them what was happening. "Go on ahead," she whisper-yelled. "We'll catch up to you!"

Marilyn and Kevan quickly disappeared around the corner as Alicia's phone made a soft chime sound.

"What's it say?" Kathy asked.

After a slight pause and a look of confusion, Alicia turned the screen of her phone around to show Kathy.

The text read, "'I took dad phone to text you. He look at spaceships on video. He say they are in air now.'" And after Kathy read it out loud, she gasped. "Wow. He's really good at texting."

"My dad's on the Internet looking up flying saucers?" Alicia asked, not believing what she was asking.

"That's what it sounds like," Kathy admitted gravely. "Maybe he's searching the Internet for any recent UFO sightings ... eyewitness videos and stuff like that."

"This is crazy, Kathy."

"Well, it makes perfect sense. Your dad has to know he's been working for vampires. And it also sounds like he knows they're from another planet."

Alicia started to bite her lip.

"Which also means that he might know what's about to happen to Earth."

Alicia stared blankly ahead, trying to piece things together. "He refuses to go to the drive-in tonight. Kevan knew the film had secret messages ... Kevan says my dad was helping them restore the film, but I still don't think he knows anything. I mean, this is my dad we're talking about. Not some kind of a spy."

"Ask Jimmy—"

"The film's gone!" Kevan cried out in a panic. He was running as fast as he could toward them, with the storage room key dangling in his hand.

Kathy cringed. "What?!"

Marilyn flew around the corner, hovering in the air right behind Kevan, her face filled with frustration. "I wish we'd known about this film and its secret messages earlier."

"Where do you think it went?!" Kathy asked Kevan.

Kevan looked at Alicia and pointed. "I think her dad has it."

Harold Chavez trembled and shivered, wrapped inside a fuzzy blue blanket, scared out of his mind. The blanket had a lot of bright yellow rubber duckies on it, but that didn't seem to comfort him very much. He was curled up into a ball on the living room couch. In front of him, a large TV screen with colorful cartoons that seemed to go on endlessly. It was on the same channel Jimmy had left it on before he snuck his father's phone into his bag, and was taken to school, and as much as Harold wanted to change the channel, he was too afraid to move. He was petrified.

He'd slammed his laptop shut about twenty minutes earlier and safely abandoned it in the kitchen. At that moment, he never wanted to look at it again. It had frightened him more than he had ever been frightened by anything in his entire life, and he contemplated throwing it into the trash. He even considered dunking it into the toilet first, but then realized it wouldn't fit inside the bowl. Those spaceships ... hovering up there ... waiting. He'd seen it with his own eyes. There were already several videos of them on the Internet ... well, blurry videos. But that was all Harold needed to see. He knew something wasn't right. And it wasn't just him ... other people knew about them, too. There were other believers out there—vigilant, curious citizens with video cameras who knew that something wasn't right with the night skies over San Antonio, Texas.

*It can't be real. This can't be happening.*

Immediately after slamming the laptop shut, Harold took to pacing around the house for a little while, looking for his phone. He wanted to call his wife at work, so he could let her know about the videos he'd seen. Harold knew how she'd react at first. She would act like he was insane. She would ask him exactly where he'd seen these videos and would remind him how so many videos with UFOs in them were faked. Harold would agree with her, be told to find something else to do, and then he'd end the phone call and think about spaceships anyway … and that strange thing that happened to him last night …

*What?!* Harold suddenly (and accidentally) remembered in fear—but only in foggy bits and pieces.

Harold reached up to feel his teeth. *Nothing sharp or pointy.* Good. But he still had his suspicions. He remembered a mist and a pale face … Harold pulled the blanket up and over his head. He remembered an arm reaching out for him in the kitchen. *Nooooooo!!!*

And he remembered asking a question to a pair of red beady eyes.

"Am I turning into a vampire?"

The red eyes, enveloped within a darkness that was enveloped inside a thick, swirly mist answered, "What are you talking about?"

"Why do you keep visiting me like this?"

"Here," the voice answered flatly. An arm wrapped in black, reached out from inside the mist to hand Harold a bag with film canisters inside. "You must keep this at your house until we come back for it tomorrow night."

"What is it?"

"The film."

"But why? I took it to the school like you asked me to."

"Because the school isn't a safe enough place for it any longer." The voice sounded different, maybe European. And it sounded sort of annoyed also. "Why do you ask so many questions? Just do what I say!"

Harold cowered down and averted his eyes from the mist. "Okay," he replied weakly. "So just to be clear about things ... I'm not turning into a vampire?"

"No, silly man. I make you hungry each night so we can meet in your kitchen to discuss the film. Calm down," the foreign-sounding voice said to him. "And don't look up any UFO videos on the Internet."

"Why not?"

"Because I said so!" the voice demanded. "Geez. How come nobody listens to me?!"

Harold shook his head and forced himself to stop remembering. Then he gasped in disbelief. *Oh no! It's here ... the film is here ... in this house!*

# Chapter 14

They had to formulate a plan, and they had to do it quickly. Kathy and Alicia eagerly volunteered to take the rest of the school day off to help locate the missing film, but Marilyn was adamantly against it. She wanted the girls in class, and she wanted Kevan to do anything he could to find out more about the missing film from his family.

And so, naturally, Kevan agreed. His plan was to head back to his uncle's spaceship, casually ask him about his plans for the film, and report to Marilyn with the details as quickly as possible. And while Kevan did this, Marilyn would head over to Alicia's house to check on her father. Perhaps she could persuade Harold Chavez to tell her where the film might be, since Kevan was convinced that Alicia's dad knew something more about it than he was letting on to. However, like usual, there was a problem with their plan.

"Ally's dad can't see you," Kathy reminded her aunt as they hurried down the hall. "He isn't a believer, remember?"

Marilyn scoffed. "He believes in vampires, why not ghosts?"

"Isn't there a way you can still communicate with him?" Kevan asked her. "Maybe you could haunt him ... move things around in the house to get his attention?"

"Oh no," Marilyn replied, waving her hands in front of her. "That would be too scary for him. I think he's been through enough this week."

"Then what are you going to do?" Alicia asked.

Marilyn stopped in her tracks, and they all looked at her expectantly. "If I can't get him to see me in solid form, I'm going to look around the house for that film. And if I can't find it, I'll text you and Kathy."

Kevan scanned Marilyn, wondering something about her transparency. "If you can turn solid, why wouldn't he see you? And how will you text Kathy? Do you have a ghost phone or something?"

Marilyn smiled. "I can't be seen in solid form unless the person seeing me believes in ghosts ... or at least the possibility of them. And I can text with my mind. It's like a ghost-network. Don't vampires do the same thing?"

"I use a universal phone. Haven't developed my psychic abilities very well yet, but my uncle's great at it—"

"Excuse me," Kathy interrupted. "Planet Earth needs us. You can compare mind powers later."

"Oh, right!" Marilyn giggled and turned back toward Kevan. "You know what to do, young man. Be safe and don't get caught. We believe in you."

Then, with a big smile and a misty poof, she was gone.

"Your aunt's cool," Kevan said to Kathy.

"Thanks. Now how are you getting up to that spaceship your uncle's on?"

"I have my ways," he answered confidently. Kevan adjusted the strap of the backpack on his shoulder. "You two need to get back to class. Don't worry. I have your phone numbers. If I need to, I'll text you."

Kevan turned and jogged down the hallway, leaving the girls to wonder if there was anything they could do to help—besides going to class.

"I'm late for a quiz," Alicia groaned. "I don't know how I'm going to concentrate with all of this going on."

Kathy understood how she felt. It was a helpless, guilty sort of feeling that stuck to you like an old, forgotten stepped on piece of food from the cafeteria. "It's up to them now. Marilyn knows what she's doing."

The Chavez house looked very peaceful from where Marilyn stood on the front porch. There didn't seem to be anything noticeably out of order — other than the complete and utter silence that surrounded it.

"That's odd," she thought out loud. "No birds singing, no breeze blowing ... nothing."

She leaned in to peek through the decorative glass window on the door. On the inside, Alicia's house looked just like Alicia's house should have looked. Marilyn could make out the edge of a couch and could see a large attractive vase sitting on the living room floor next to a fireplace. On the back window, dark-blue curtains hung in a way to allow just the right amount of light in. There was a large flat-screen television attached to the wall above the fireplace, glowing in flashes of bright animated colors, which didn't seem strange at all to Marilyn until a figure with a pronounced hunch in its back, draped in all black, appeared to glide across the floor just beneath it.

Marilyn quickly ducked away from the window. Her eyes were wide, surprised at what she had seen. It was most certainly a vampire … unless Alicia's dad had a long black cape and didn't care much about his posture in recent days. She took shallow breaths, contemplating her next move.

There was the distinct sound of a bang inside the house. Marilyn flinched, caught her breath, and then dared herself to peek again into the house. She had to be careful because she knew vampires could see ghosts just as well as she could see vampires.

She went as transparent as possible, her head inching across the window. There was no sign of movement and no noise. And so Marilyn decided to push her way through the front door, head first, but slowly, so that no electrical disturbances, not even on a microscopic level, could be detected by anyone sensitive enough to feel them. After passing through the door, she edged herself along the wall until she heard something … ice clanking around in a glass?

"Do you understand my instructions?" A deep voice with a distinct accent asked.

The clanking sound grew louder. "Yes," a man answered nervously. "But I honestly don't know where the film is."

Upon hearing this, Marilyn sank into the wall behind her.

"I will help you remember when the time is right," the deep voice said. "For now, I want to ask you a few questions."

Marilyn pushed her misty face through the living room wall. She did this so carefully, enough to see them, and not enough to be seen. And then she saw him—it was Sir Ghoulingheart. Alicia's father shivered in fear on the couch, clutching a glass of ice water in his hands as Sir Ghoulingheart stood over him.

Then, the intimidating vampire leaned in close to Harold's face. "Someone's been investigating me."

A thick knot formed inside Marilyn's throat.

Harold squirmed in his seat. He tightened the blanket around himself. "I don't know what you're talking about."

Sir Ghoulingheart sneered at him. "You have a daughter, don't you, Mr. Chavez?"

Harold trembled when he responded, "Yes."

"And she attends the school that we are so graciously screening our film to tonight."

"Yes, she does." Harold looked confused and extremely frightened.

"Mr. Preston, your boss, has a daughter who also attends that very same school."

"Yes, I know. The girls have been good friends ever since the Preston family moved here months ago."

Sir Ghoulingheart took a step back and dramatically soured his face. "Kathy Preston is a problem, Mr. Chavez."

"She is?"

"Of all the schools on Earth, I choose the school Kathy Preston attends."

Harold looked at the vampire innocently. "What's wrong with that? It's just a vintage movie, right?"

Sir Ghoulingheart seemed to look right through him as he spoke. "You still have no idea what you've done. This proves how talented I am with memory spells."

Harold frowned in confusion.

"But I was still unaware that Mark Preston was Kathy Preston's father."

Harold curled back into the couch.

"Listen!" the vampire yelled angrily. "I chose McDaniels, Daniels and Sons Technologies to help restore my film for a reason. I chose them because they are very good at what they do, very efficient, and because I had secretly worked with them before in a city nearby called Houston when Mr. Preston was employed at that location. He had no knowledge about my true identity, nor did he pry into it or care. He wanted my business—no matter *what* I was. To him, I was Mr. Fuller from California, and Mr. Fuller had limitless amounts of Earth money. That's all he needed to know. You see?"

"Y-Yes."

"I give Mr. Preston money, and Mr. Preston does what I say. That's good customer service!"

Harold answered with a tremor in his voice, "Yes, It's a great company and I really enjoy working there—"

"But I had no idea that Kathy Preston was his daughter!"

Harold recoiled again and forced a smile on his face—the kind of smile that begged for forgiveness. "I don't understand why that's a problem."

Sir Ghoulingheart's chest began to heave angrily. He leaned over Harold, threateningly, and snarled intensely into his face. "This Kathy has an aunt who is connected with a very dreadful, nosy organization that wishes to prevent my fellow creatures from winning the many, many big shiny trophies that we so rightfully deserve."

Marilyn pulled her face back into the wall and placed a hand delicately over her mouth. She was frozen, afraid to make a single sound.

"This organization—which is too horrible to speak the name of because it will make my stomach turn at the sound of it—," the vampire continued, "was careless enough to run my name, my brother's name, and my nephew's name through an inter-universal computer database. They were trying to gather information about us. Trying to see what we've been up to. Scouring and creeping around our car club's members-only website!"

Harold only nodded, pretending to understand what the scary vampire in his living room was going on about.

"And do you know *how* I know that they were doing this?"

"Uh ... a spy told you?"

"No! That is ridiculous! Why do you say such mindless things to me?!"

Harold gulped. "I'm sorry."

"I know what they were doing because I signed up for an anti-identity theft membership only a few short moons ago! That's how!" Sir Ghoulingheart placed his hands firmly on his hips and stood proud, tipping his chin into the air. "I'm sure you would not understand since nobody would possibly want to steal *your* identity. You would not believe how many beings in this universe wish that they could be me! If I wasn't me, I would steal my *own* identity! So of course I have to keep track of these types of things. If anyone looks into my background deeply enough on any computer in any universe ... I will find out!"

Marilyn closed her eyes and wished that she, and The Order, had been more careful about checking into the Ghoulingheart vampires.

Harold squirmed again. Whatever the vampire was saying made no sense to him. The project was finished. He'd completed his end of the bargain. "I finished the film. I did everything you instructed me to do ... even though I don't remember half of what you told me—"

"That's because I hypnotized your weak mind! I made you forget!" Sir Ghoulingheart hissed callously.

"Uh ... okay," Harold said, feeling more than a little insulted. "What I was trying to say before you interrupted me, was that I did what you told me to do. I don't know what else you could possibly want from me. So," Harold continued in much less of a submissive tone than before, "could you please stop visiting me here at my house?"

"No."

"What? Why?"

"Trust me, visiting you is not something I look forward to. But because I have had to change some of my plans unexpectedly, here I am." Sir Ghoulingheart rolled his eyes.

"Please," Harold begged, "just take the film. I have no idea where it is because I don't remember where you told me to hide it, but I'm sure it's here somewhere!"

Sir Ghoulingheart, quite impressed with his ability to scare humans until they broke down in front of him, released a dark laugh. "We are going to check the girls out of school. They will have doctors' appointments or something like that."

"What?!"

The vampire looked upward, then nodded and pointed a finger into the air before saying, "Activate now," before returning his attention back to the human in front of him. "And, because I know we are being watched by a special visitor, I have just placed a psi-shield around this house."

There was a sudden look of terror in Marilyn's eyes.

"You see, Mr. Chavez," the amused vampire began, "you have an intruder in your home."

"Who? *You*?"

"No, silly man! Another intruder. A ghost woman!" Sir Ghoulingheart curled his hand into a wicked fist and glared through the wall—straight into Marilyn's glassy eyes. "It is Marilyn Preston! And now she is trapped inside this house!"

"Oh," Harold replied quietly. "A ghost. Okay."

The vampire gazed deep into Harold's eyes and commanded, "Let's get those girls. They're going to be late for their doctors' appointments."

Harold rose from the couch and stared blankly ahead, the ducky blanket still draped around his shoulders.

"And take off that baby cape! I cannot be seen in public with you looking like that!"

Marilyn drew in a deep breath and then stepped out from inside the wall and into view. Sir Ghoulingheart only acknowledged her with a sidelong glance and a dismissive smile as he grabbed Alicia's dad by the arm and dragged him toward the front door. "Good luck trying to contact your Mystical Order for help, ghost woman. The psychic shield I have beaming down from my ship will not allow it. Any thought-messages you send out for help will be pointless. This drive-in is just the beginning! Soon, Condemned Vampire Cookout will be screened all over the world!"

Marilyn sharpened her stare on him and in a threatening voice warned, "You'd better stay away from those girls, Vilester!"

The vampire opened a closet door just inside the entrance of the house and reached above several hanging jackets for a bag containing four old rusty film canisters. The bag had been sitting on a shelf, just high enough and out of sight, since the night before. He clutched the bag close to his chest and smiled back at Marilyn. "You lose, Ms. Preston. After tonight, Earth will never be the same."

# Chapter 15

The Sinatra Middle School principal's office smelled like cotton candy most of the time. That was because the principal, Mrs. Barrett, liked it that way. She had one of those fancy wax burners in her office and a small drawer filled with various wax scents to melt inside it whenever she pleased. On the walls hung pictures of the school's football, volleyball, track, dance, and other teams from years past. So when one of the star varsity football players asked if he could speak with her, she only hoped that it wasn't about anything too serious as she rushed from the faculty breakroom to her office. The office receptionist had made it clear that the young man seemed very worried about something. She'd even asked him if he needed to visit the nurse instead, but he refused.

As Mrs. Barrett arrived, she smiled nervously at the receptionist and fumbled with her glasses. A few students helping in the main office stood at attention upon seeing their principal, but she was too distracted. She didn't even notice them. Mrs. Barrett pointed at her office door, and the receptionist nodded in return.

The receptionist rose from her desk, straightening out the sleeves of her blouse. "He looks a little ... shaken," she whispered.

"Shaken?" the principal asked.

"Yes. And he refused to see the nurse."

The principal frowned, and because she felt completely lost and helpless in the situation, she stared blankly before asking, "And he says he saw a strange animal?"

The receptionist scanned their surroundings before answering, "I think you'd better hear it from him." She then pointed behind her at the principal's office door.

Mrs. Barrett adjusted her glasses and the heart-shaped pendant on her silver necklace, then forced a smile. She took a few steps toward her office door, hoping that she wouldn't be calling any animal rescue people into the building, or that rumors wouldn't get out about a raccoon or a possum ... she turned the doorknob and bravely entered her office.

Adam Mendez turned in his seat to greet her.

"Hello, Mrs. Barrett. Sorry to be missing class like this, but—"

"It's okay, Adam," Mrs. Barrett replied in a cheerful voice. "Any time a student is in need, I'm here for them. You know that. I hope everything is well."

"Oh, yes," he answered shakily. "Um … but I did have a question for you, and I didn't want to ask Mr. Science guy … uh, I meant Mr. Morton. Actually, I didn't really know who to go to about it."

Mrs. Barrett moved carefully around her desk to take her seat, ducking underneath the scraggly long arms of a hanging plant in the process. "You came to the right person. What's your question?"

Adam tilted his head and stared at the plant for a moment, wondering if it was plastic, then realizing that it wasn't. The extra-green plant was just really healthy-looking. "Are bats supposed to talk?"

"Bats?"

"Yeah. Like the ones that fly around and hang upside down and stuff. I don't know much about them, but … they don't speak, right?"

Mrs. Barrett looked over her glasses at him. "Did you see a bat inside the school?"

"Yes."

"Where?"

"In the locker room."

"When?"

Adam hesitated. "This morning. After practice."

Mrs. Barrett rubbed her hands together. "And you *spoke* to it?"

"No," the student answered simply. "It spoke to *me*."

Mrs. Barrett half-stood from her chair, looking over Adam's arms and face with concern before sitting back down. "Did it bite you?"

"No."

"Adam," she began, "bats can be very dangerous. They might look like cute little creatures, but some of them—not all—but some of them, can be very harmful to people. You didn't touch it, did you?"

Adam answered innocently, "No."

Mrs. Barrett was puzzled, a little bewildered, and also slightly confused with Adam's story. Yes, she was concerned that there might be a bat inside the school, but she was more concerned with the fact that one of her star football players had claimed to have heard it speak to him. "So it squeaked at you?"

Adam thought on the question for a moment,

his mouth hanging open. "Yeah … it did squeak a few times. After it asked me for some help."

Mrs. Barrett contorted her face in a way that would be best described as in between surprise and horror. "It asked you for help?"

"It wanted me to hand it a backpack."

Mrs. Barrett contemplated this in silence, even imagining it a little.

"The backpack was on the floor, and the bat was kinda floating above it." Adam placed his hand in front of him at eye level. "Like, right here."

"Was it *your* backpack?"

"No. I think it was his. I'm pretty sure it was a boy bat. You know, since it was in the boys' locker room and all that."

"Are you sure you don't want to go speak to the nurse or anything … right now?"

"No. Actually, I feel a lot better now that I talked to you about this," Adam said to her. "I just wanted to let you know about the talking bat."

"Oh." Mrs. Barrett really didn't know what to say or how to react. "I'll have one of the custodians look in the boys' locker room in case it's still in there."

"It left."

"Left?!"

"Yeah. It asked me to open the door that goes outside." Adam pointed a finger into the air above his head. "It took its backpack and … went up."

"Up?"

"Yeah." Adam smiled. "He flew out the door and went up and up and up … he just kept going until I couldn't see him anymore."

Mrs. Barrett looked rather disturbed by this. She leaned back into her seat and stared at Adam, unsure of what to say next.

"Thanks, Mrs. B," Adam said. "I feel much better now. I think I'll go back to class."

"Wait!" she cried out with a start. "You're telling me that a tiny little bat carried a backpack up into the air?"

"He could talk, so maybe he had magical powers."

Mrs. Barrett gritted her teeth. "I don't think you should tell anyone else about this. Especially students."

Adam tightened his lips and looked away from her.

"Did you tell anyone besides me, Adam?"

"I posted something about it online," he admitted as he struggled to pull his phone out of his pocket, "but I can delete it if you think … oh. It has, like, 248 likes already."

Mrs. Barrett, now extremely frustrated, decided to shake the whole thing off with a frantic, twitchy nod. She jumped up from her seat and motioned for Adam to do the same. "I have an idea! Just tell everyone the post was a joke!"

"Yeah. Okay."

Mrs. Barrett opened her office door and put on a weak smile. "Go back to class, Adam. I'll come by and check on you later."

"Thanks, Mrs. B," he replied, leaving her office with some confidence in his steps.

Principal Barrett slowly closed her office door, still envisioning the bat Adam had described to her. She saw a quick image of it in her head, fluttering around the locker room. Then she imagined how it might look if it spoke. This made her laugh, in short bursts at first and then heartily. Mrs. Barrett laughed so hard that she staggered backward until she slammed into the front of her desk, causing everything on top of it to rattle and shake. "Oops!"

Embarrassed, she immediately looked up at her office door, hoping that no one had heard how clumsy she'd been. Mrs. Barrett gasped. She locked her eyes onto a piece of bright green paper taped to the back of the door — it was a flyer made by the student council advertising that evening's family movie night.

"Bats, huh?" the principal smiled wide. "I think," she said with a giggle, "Coach Hansen and the football team are playing a practical joke on me."

Principal Barrett burst into laughter again and grabbed onto her desk to keep herself from falling to the floor in hysterics.

30 minutes later.

Kathy stared at the clock above her math teacher's head. Her backpack was on the floor next to her feet. It had been strategically placed, half open, so she could peek at the screen of her phone as needed—but her phone hadn't received a single message since class began. Not one from Marilyn, not one from Alicia, and not a single one from Kevan.

Her teacher was going on about finances and how essential math would be in their lives as productive adult members of society. And since texting wasn't allowed in class, Kathy just had to sit there and wait. As soon as a message came in, she was going to covertly slip her phone into her jean jacket, excuse herself to the restroom, and help coordinate the rest of their mission from there. Because that's exactly what it had become to her—a mission. A duty she had been enlisted to serve, in an effort to stand up for, and protect, her fellow students.

Kathy looked up as she realized that her teacher had stopped talking. A student helper from the office had popped his head in through the door, holding a small piece of paper in his hand. Kathy knew that small pink rectangular paper well, every student did. It was their ticket out of class.

"Kathy Preston?" her teacher called out.

There was disappointment on the other students' faces.

"Yes?"

"You're needed at the front office. Please take your things with you," her teacher said. He fumbled with some things on his desk while waiting for Kathy to collect her belongings.

As Kathy approached the front of the class to leave, the student helper, a thin-framed boy with blond messy-on-purpose hair and a shy smile, stuck his arm farther into the room to hand Kathy the pink paper. Kathy took the paper from the boy's hand and proceeded to study it.

"Doctor's appointment?" she asked. "What for?"

"Miss Preston," her teacher said impatiently.

"Please report to the office so I can get back to teaching. Thank you."

"Yes, sir." And with that, Kathy left her math class and headed toward the office, the thin-framed boy walking on ahead of her as if it was a race. "Who's picking me up? She decided to ask him.

"I don't know. I think it's your dad."

"Oh."

The boy made a sharp turn around a corner, heading toward the English department.

"The office is this way," Kathy said, pointing straight ahead.

"I know," the boy answered. "But I have to deliver an early release slip for Alicia Chavez, too."

Kathy gasped abruptly, but then quickly corrected herself. And then she said, as if disinterested, "That's interesting. *Very* interesting."

# Chapter 16

I t was easy for Kevan to sneak back onto his uncle's spaceship. Hovering many miles above Earth, the ship's occupants — several other vampires — were busy preparing for that evening's event. Vashmirian vamps bustled about the main garage area making last-minute adjustments to their suped up cars and trucks. Because it was so busy, Kevan knew that the main garage would be the best part of the ship to sneak back into. In all the frenzy, he would blend right in.

So in a dark corner, Kevan discreetly popped into the ship, still in the form of a bat, and somehow, with his tiny little bat hands, held onto his favorite Earth-style backpack. Earth backpacks were the latest trend with teens around the universe. They could be decorated with patches and buttons from his favorite bands. It was far better than the traditional vampire carriers his father preferred to use. Kevan found those bags to be bulky, sharp, and spikey in all the wrong places. They weren't made of any type of material you could stick pins into or sew patches on either. In fact, the only benefit vampire carriers did have was that they could turn into a vaporous mist when needed. Earth backpacks couldn't do that.

Kevan ducked his bat body down behind a cherry red coupe and hovered just low enough to survey the goings-on inside the garage. The backpack was getting heavy, but he couldn't let go of it. Inside the bag was the film—all four canisters containing the original version of Condemned Vampire Cookout—the version *without* the secret messages on it. Kevan concentrated, focused hard, and then transformed himself back into a teen boy. *I need to find my father*, he thought. So He pulled the strap of his backpack over his shoulder and glanced into the side mirror of the car to check his hair. Upon seeing his reflection—which of course, he could see even though he was a vampire— Kevan contorted his face and quickly used his fingers to twist and pull parts of his hair back up into the messier look he preferred it to be in. *And I need to find some hair gel*.

A commanding voice boomed over all the others in the garage, halting every busy vampire in his or her tracks. "I have received a message from my brother, Sir Ghoulingheart," the voice stated dramatically. It was Kevan's father, Shawn.

Kevan lowered himself down again and watched his father through the car's windows. His father stood tall and proud, more confident than usual. Every vampire remained still, their attention focused only on Shawn as they waited for him to speak again.

Shawn lifted his chin into the air. "We will proceed as planned," he said calmly. "My brother wants every vampire assigned to tonight's mission to be dressed in jeans ... no capes!"

There were some murmurs of disappointment.

"Leather jackets are okay, but the important part is to blend in with the Earth people on this mission ... and to be sure that your cars have been cleaned and tuned appropriately," Shawn reminded them.

A few of the vampires leaning against the walls smiled and nodded upon hearing this. And the smiles were quite sinister-looking.

"We only have eight Earth hours before this mission begins." Shawn looked extremely serious. "My fellow vampires, although this is considered a test mission, its success is vital to the future of our people. Once the humans see the film, they will be intrigued and entranced by it … then they will feel compelled to tell others about what they have seen and learned. They will search for it online … and while this is happening, we will then prepare for the next showings of Condemned Vampire Cookout all across the planet!"

Kevan watched as vampire mechanics smiled and nodded at one another, looking very satisfied by what his father was saying.

Shawn looked around, frowning. "Has anyone seen my son?"

None of the vampires had seen Kevan, so many of them shook their heads.

"Ah," Shawn replied. "Well, if he shows up, please tell him that I am looking for him. Now, return to your tasks!"

Kevan cringed and slowly stood as his father turned to leave the garage. Vampires immediately went back to clinking and clanking on things as they were instructed. Kevan inhaled a deep breath, the overwhelming smell of motor oil and gasoline filling his nostrils. He knew it was time to face his father.

"Hi there, Kevan!" a woman's voice said. She had long black hair and was holding a welder's mask in her hand. "Your dad's looking for you."

"Oh," Kevan said, trying to sound surprised.

"Thanks."

The woman smiled and walked away. Kevan's shoulders sank. He made his way out from behind the cherry red car and headed toward the closest exit. His heart was pounding and he kept his head low, hoping not to be recognized by any other adult vampires. But since he was the only teenager on board the ship, that would prove to be impossible.

"Hi, Kevan!"

"Hi, Mrs. Spikelton."

"Hey, Kevan. Your pop wants to—"

"Yeah. I know. Thanks, Mr. Finkelbert."

"Kevan! There you are! Your dad—"

"Yes, thanks, Mr. Van Gassel. I know."

And when Kevan made it to the exit, he sighed and pushed open the door. His father was standing in the hallway waiting for him, the look on his face blank and unreadable. This made Kevan very nervous since an unreadable expression could mean many things when coming from a parent.

"Hello, father," Kevan began. "I heard you've been looking for me."

Heavy creases formed on his father's forehead. "Where have you been?" he asked sternly.

"On Earth."

"Having conversations with Earth teenagers?"

Kevan avoided his father's intimidating stare. "Just a little."

"I need to have a serious talk with you, but I am limited on time," his father said.

"Because you're busy getting things ready for tonight, right?"

His father eyed him suspiciously. "Yes."

"Can I help?"

Shawn's eyes went wide. "Help? You haven't helped with a single part of this mission. What makes you want to help us now? Only hours before we land?"

A dozen excuses rushed through Kevan's head, but he had only moments to settle on one. "I don't know."

"Let's have a seat in our quarters. We need to have a talk before your Uncle Vilester comes back."

"A talk about what, Dad?"

His father turned his back to him before answering, and proceeded to walk ahead of him down the long hallway. "About movie night."

Kevan and his father shared a very large room on the ship. Great care had been taken in furnishing and decorating it. It had a very gloomy, but sophisticated feel. There were ornate, dark wooden chairs, some as large as thrones. The floor was lined with soft rugs that were deep red in color. And although there had been numerous electric light fixtures installed throughout, Shawn preferred the warm, classic glow of candles.

"Have a seat, son," his father instructed kindly.

Kevan set his backpack on the ground and sat in an oversized chair facing his father. Between them was an ancient-looking trunk with a few glowing candles on top. Behind his father, on top of an old armoire, several other candles flickered, adding to the ambiance.

Kevan's father crossed his arms. "I fought very hard to bring you along with me on this trip to Earth. Your uncle was against it."

Kevan grumbled, "Because he hates me."

"No. Because he knew you wouldn't understand the point of the mission."

Kevan tried, but couldn't hold it back any longer. He just had to ask. "What's going on with the film? Why did Vile have secret messages put on it? What's going to happen to the people who watch it?!"

His father leaned back in his seat, the light from the candles creating deep shadows that appeared to dance slowly across his face. "Hundreds of years ago, a group of vampires came to this planet," he said, pointing a finger toward the floor, "to look around and explore. But they were not careful."

"What do you mean?"

"They were seen," his father answered, "by humans."

"Oh."

"Villagers talked about the vampires and feared them." His father's expression grew dark before continuing. "Our people come from a gruesome past, as all people do. But at that time, the way our people behaved, and ate in the forests, and how we must have looked while doing so, frightened these Earth villagers … it frightened the hunters in the woods. So they went back to their families empty handed, without meals for their people … because they had been scared out of the forests by what they had seen. This caused a problem for us."

Kevan seemed confused by this revelation. "Why was it a problem for us? The hunters saw our people, got scared, and ran away … but we look so much like humans. Do we really look that scary when we eat?" His mind was racing. "What happened next?"

"The hunters were too afraid to venture back

into the forests. And the villagers would hardly come out of their homes." Kevan's father stared into his son's eyes. "Do you understand why this was a bad thing?"

"Not really. Our people didn't attack them, did they?"

"No. But they did see our people hunting the same animals that they hunted. This should not have happened. Our people should not have been seen, nor should they have been taking food from the Earth people," his father answered. "It started rumors. Neighboring villages were afraid, too."

Kevan was now very interested in his father's story. "Then what happened?"

"Well," his father began, "because we are not allowed to disturb any planet that we visit, we had to repair the situation. Our people had to reverse the damage that was done."

Kevan only nodded, intrigued with every word his father spoke.

"One of our people was given the assignment to go into a village late at night and pretend to attack a human. Once the human was in his arms, he was instructed to confess what our weaknesses were."

"No!" Kevan reacted quickly. "He gave away our secrets?!"

"Of course not!" Shawn laughed. "Not the *real* ones."

Kevan relaxed again and listened.

"We gave them a story ... something to believe in ... something that might help them to feel powerful and strong against us." He smiled. "So because of our stories, they hung garlic outside their doors and windows and came out in the daytime thinking that the vampires could not attack them in the safety of daylight. They felt safe again. And our people immediately left their planet, hoping that the stories of the vampire would fade away gently over time ..."

Kevan shook his head. "But they didn't."

"No," his father replied in a sad voice. "No, they didn't. Mythology is a very interesting thing. The story of the vampire, instead, grew stronger. Things were added to it, and it kept on and on throughout the ages."

From the look on Shawn's face, Kevan knew that his father's story wasn't finished. Kevan waited in a polite silence for him to continue.

"That's why we are here, son. We have returned to Earth to fix things."

# Chapter 17

Kathy and Alicia walked shoulder to shoulder down the quiet hallway. As they got closer to the school's main office, a variety of theories popped in and out of Kathy's head. Since both of them were being checked out of school at the same time, it had to be a part of some coordinated plan.

Kathy brushed the bangs from her forehead. "Ally?"

"Yes?"

"Do you have a doctor's appointment today?"

Alicia puckered her lips while thinking about it. "My mom didn't say anything about one this morning."

Kathy slowed her pace. "Has Marilyn texted you?"

"No."

"She hasn't texted me either."

"Do you think she's the one checking us out of school?"

Kathy frowned. "I don't know. And I can't text her to ask. In a thought text, she can only text me. I can email her, but she only checks things like that when she's back at her office. She can't carry any electronic devices with her when she's a ghost."

The two girls slowed their pace, looking a little worried, but continued on toward the office. Until Alicia grabbed Kathy by the sleeve of her jacket.

"What?" Kathy asked.

"If we're being checked out for doctors' appointments, we have to figure out a way to get out of them!"

"I know," Kathy agreed.

"We'll have to pretend to be too sick to go!"

"That doesn't make any sense, Ally. That's like being too hungry to go eat."

"Huh?"

"Never mind."

At the end of the hallway, a man stepped into view from around the corner, his silhouette very familiar to Kathy. "It's my dad."

And as the girls got closer to the office, an eerie feeling began to brew inside them. Kathy's father wasn't smiling at them. Instead, was a chilling blank stare. Alicia glanced at Kathy's face for a reaction and was confused by what she saw — Kathy was smiling a very fake-looking smile at her father in return.

"Are you okay?" Alicia asked.

Kathy's smile got bigger. "Sure. Why not?"

"Your dad doesn't look right," she replied.

"Neither does yours."

Alicia stopped in her tracks, her mouth dropping open at the sight of her father. Now both in full view, the two dads seemed a bit off. And when I say a bit, I actually mean a lot. Because unlike zombies that are crooked, sometimes drooling, and even somewhat crumbly — Alicia and Kathy's fathers were, instead, blank and stale. There was something missing in their faces — that dad-like quality that the girls were familiar with.

But Kathy's fake smile remained strong. "Hi, Dad."

"Hello, daughter," he replied in a monotone, empty sort of way. "We will be leaving the school now. There is an appointment. One for each of you."

Alicia's father, disheveled and now twitching as he was about to speak, stepped in closer to them. "We are running late, girls."

"Hold on," Kathy said. "We *both* have appointments at the same time? For what?"

Kathy's father raised his eyebrows. "For the doctor."

"What doctor?"

"The one ... with ... the office in that building with the windows on it, darling," he replied slowly. "And he's waiting for us. It's time to go." He reached out for her.

Kathy took a step backward. "An eye doctor, or —?"

"Excuse me," Alicia boldly interrupted. "Both of us have appointments with the same doctor?"

"We're carpooling," her father answered.

Alicia looked at Kathy, wanting her to see the fear in her eyes, but also wanting to hide it from their fathers. And although Kathy only acknowledged it with a slight nod, she felt the same sort of fear. It was the kind of fear you feel when something you know and trust suddenly changes. So Kathy had to think quickly. "We have an important test today."

"It can be rescheduled," her father replied flatly. He looked around and then leaned in and lowered his voice. "Your aunt sent us to pick you up. We need to hurry."

Kathy looked at Alicia's dad, noticing the way he seemed to be hypnotically staring through the back of her father's head. "Okay, I guess we should go," she said cheerily.

"We *should*?" Alicia asked.

"Yes. Of course we should," she said while carefully reaching into her jacket.

Kathy's father looked back at Alicia's father, smiling wide. "You see, Harold? I told you that taking the girls to their doctors' appointments together would be fun. Maybe afterward we can all go out for some ice cream. That is what you people like to do, isn't it?"

"I prefer vanilla," Kathy replied while busily typing into her phone.

Her father stared at the phone in her hands, his eyes becoming a bit concerned. "What are you doing?"

"Texting," she replied as she pressed send.

His eyes blinked rapidly. "Texting?"

"Yes. I'm texting you." Kathy placed a hand on her hip, smiled a most genuine smile, and waited. She waited for a reaction to come from the man standing before her, and also waited for the phone in her hand to notify her of an incoming text — and it did so very quickly. And when Kathy's phone illuminated, Alicia peeked over to look at the screen. The text read, "I'm at work. Why?"

The face of the man standing in front of her went cold. His eyes swelled with rage, and his hands formed into tightly clenched fists. Kathy stepped back, reached over for Alicia, and grabbed ahold of her by the sleeve.

"Give me your phone, Kathryn," the man standing before them instructed in a dark, heavy accent. "Now."

Alicia's lips quivered. "What's going on?"

"That's not my dad," Kathy answered. But what made that statement more confusing than it already sounded, was the fact that the man she was referring to still looked exactly like her father. "We have to get out of here. We have to find Marilyn."

The man pointed a finger into the air. "Interesting that you should mention her."

"Why?" Kathy asked fearfully. "What have you done to her?"

"And what have you done to my dad?" Alicia wondered.

"If you'd like to keep your aunt safe, Kathryn, then I suggest you come with me," the man growled. "And as for your father, Alicia, I am certainly beginning to enjoy having an assistant. I am such a busy man ... I'm thinking about *keeping* him."

"No!" Alicia cried out.

He let out a most fiendish laugh.

Alicia's father continued on staring at the back of Kathy's fake-father's head, as if awaiting his next command. Kathy resisted the urge to scream for help. There was no telling what would happen anyway if she did. Kathy had a good idea about who this man really was. He could take on her father's appearance and had done a decent job of copying his voice. And if she was correct about her assumption, the entire school could be in danger if she and Alicia didn't handle things smoothly.

She remained calm. "Where's my aunt?"

The man grinned. "Come with me and I'll show you."

"Are you Sir Ghoulingheart?"

The man seemed to enjoy hearing the sound of his own name very much. "Yes, I am."

Alicia shuddered.

"If we go with you, will you let Alicia's dad go?" Kathy asked.

"No, Kathy!" Alicia begged, pulling on Kathy's sleeve, trying to make eye contact with her, wanting to tell her with her eyes that they should run, that they could escape if they tried. They were so close to a fire exit ...

"If I said yes, I would be lying," Sir Ghoulingheart admitted. "Sorry."

Kathy looked at Alicia and instantly understood her plan—but unfortunately, so did

Sir Ghoulingheart.

"I can read your minds," he reminded them. "Sometimes it's more difficult for me since every species is different, but when emotions are strong—especially emotions like fear—I can read them very well."

The girls felt defeated.

Sir Ghoulingheart tilted his chin back—which was, technically, still in the shape of Kathy's father's chin—and set his eyes into a most threatening stare. "And if you do not go with me," he began to explain, "you will never see your nosy aunt again."

Kathy's heart pounded and ached inside her chest. And in her own weakness, she made the mistake of envisioning Marilyn doubled over in pain, alone someplace dark and scary ... crying out for her. "Tell me what you've done to her."

"Her energy is slowly being drained away. Everything that she needs to exist as a ghost has been cut off."

"What does that mean?!" Alicia asked forcefully.

"A psychic shield had been placed over her." Sir Ghoulingheart smiled when he said this, fangs now beginning to appear from within what still looked like Kathy's father's mouth. "Without a connection to the rest of the universe's energy, she will disintegrate into nothingness and cease to be."

"That's not true!" Kathy yelled.

Sir Ghoulingheart softly placed a finger over his lips. "Shhhh." He scanned the hallway. "You know it to be true. She is pure energy, and that is all. And once that energy is gone, so is she. If you come with me quietly, you may have a chance to save her."

Kathy felt like collapsing to the floor, wanting to give up. Her body was going weak. She hoped that the nasty vampire was lying to them as thoughts of Marilyn's suffering invaded her brain. There was no way that Kathy would ever be able to forgive herself if Marilyn disappeared into nothingness and stopped existing. "I'm sorry, Ally," Kathy began in the frailest voice Alicia had ever heard Kathy use, "but we have to do what he says."

# CHapter 18

Hours later.

Kevan awoke in a darkened room, cloudy-headed and groggy, and with many unanswered questions stuck inside his head. He felt around, trying to figure out where he was. It certainly wasn't a coffin ... it was a rectangular bed. He was in his room, the one inside his father's quarters. He had a faint memory of his father taking him there after giving him a history lesson on vampires visiting Earth. It had been a lot to absorb, and Kevan wasn't certain how to feel anymore about his role in helping Kathy and Alicia. If his father and uncle were here to help vampires, if all they wanted to do was correct a mistake, perhaps he should respect that.

The door to the room opened, and the light stung his eyes.

"Kevan?" his father asked quietly.

"Yes, Dad," he replied, still very sleepy. "I'm awake."

"Are you hungry, son?"

Kevan squirmed under his dark-blue covers and propped himself up. "A shake sounds pretty good to me right now."

His father leaned further into the room. "I have something better than a shake."

Kevan looked at him inquisitively.

"How does a furry little bunny sound to you?"

Kevan stopped breathing for a second. "But we're not supposed to —"

"Son," his father said, relaxing his shoulders and leaning himself against the door frame, "sometimes you have to bend the rules and … live a little. So to speak." He let out a quick burst of laughter.

Kevan sat up in his bed. "Dad, is it an Earth bunny?"

His father smiled and nodded proudly.

"You told me we weren't supposed to disrupt anything on any planets we travel to. You just told me a story about how much damage something like that caused on Earth hundreds of years ago."

"It's only a few little bunny rabbits. A fresh meal like that will make you feel better than you ever have." His father stopped to shake his fist in the air above him. "You'll feel like a true vampire!"

"But you just told me that we were here to fix past mistakes! You said that our people took animals from Earth hunters and —"

"Kevan Ghoulingheart!" his father snapped. Fury bubbled in his eyes. "If we had always followed the rules, *you* would not exist!"

Kevan swallowed back the lump in his throat. He thought about the words his father had said, stunned at the possibilities and the meanings they might have. Almost too confounded to speak, he managed to ask, "What are you saying?"

His father stepped into Kevan's bedroom and shut the door behind him. Within moments, his father snapped his fingers, and the dark room was illuminated with a simple spark of fire at the tip of his finger. His father lit a candle with the glowing flame and turned to face his son.

Kevan asked, "Were you one of the vampires that visited Earth all those years ago?"

"Yes." With the candle lit behind his father, it was difficult to see him. He was covered in shadows, protected by the darkness that surrounded his face. And to Kevan, he was also hiding behind his own lies.

"Was Uncle Vile with you?"

"No. And he is very upset with me for causing so much trouble on Earth. That is why we must follow his orders and help to make things right again."

Kevan felt as if his father was trying to avoid something. "What did you mean about breaking the rules ... and about me?"

"When I was here before, and we were seen by the villagers ... I reported back to our planet for instructions on what to do. It took a lot of discussion back home, a lot of time for them to make a decision. I roamed the forests of Earth, thinking and regretting ... I met a woman."

Kevan knew. He couldn't explain how, but he knew exactly who the woman was. "My mother."

"Yes." In his father's voice was relief. He was glad to finally share with his son what he had been hiding for so many years. "I could not tell you until you were old enough."

"But I'm hundreds of years old."

"You are still very young."

Part human. But it wasn't how he felt inside. But then again, how does being human really feel? "So I'm half-human?"

"Yes and no. A vampire is a vampire. And I didn't know that you would be one until you started to grow more slowly than human children do." His father turned away, trying to shield his tears, and in the orange candlelight, Kevan could see the sadness in the profile of his father's face.

"That's why I don't remember her."

"Yes. She was human, and humans don't live as long as we do." Sadness was now beginning to look like rage. "And that is why I get so upset with these Earth movies. They infuriate me. Such abominations! Such lies! If I could have turned her, your beautiful mother, my love, into a vampire so that she could live forever, I would have! But we have no such power! Perhaps somewhere, somewhere far away, there may be vampires with that kind of power ... but not us ... not any sort of vampire I know of."

And then Kevan understood so many things that had left him empty over the years. He reached out for his father, inviting him to sit next to him on the bed. "I'm sorry, Dad."

His father stepped in closer, taking his son's hand. "You don't have the desire to join us in the garage and use tools like the other kids your age. You are not driven by the same instincts that we are. Your uncle thinks that it's because of your mother, that she is where you got your Earth-feelings from. He is afraid that you feel too much of a connection to humans."

"But why do I have to work on cars to fit in? I mean, you said it yourself ... a vampire is a vampire."

"Yes, I did," his father agreed. "Look inside yourself, Kevan. As soon as we approached this planet, your first thought was to go and look for other teenagers. *Earth* teenagers. Do you feel a greater connection with those Earth teens than with your own people? I'm worried that you may be hanging around the Earth teens too much."

"I'm not hanging around them," Kevan clarified. "I just like to watch them. They play a game called football, and they go to these buildings where they sit down and learn together. I couldn't be like them. I have to drink special shakes, and if they knew why, they'd be afraid of me."

Kevan's father patted his son on the arm and sat on the edge of the bed. "You can't help how you feel. Somewhere, deep inside that vampire heart of yours, there is something human that exists." He stopped for a moment. "Your mother was very kind. Always looking out for people ... and she didn't judge anyone by what they looked like on the outside or for the faults they had. That's why she loved me. And that's why I stayed with her and helped take care of you until it was her time to go."

Kevan held back the tears, trying to be strong for his father.

"You were a baby for a very long time," his father said with a sniffle and a smile.

"So you stayed on Earth with her ... and me? Did any of the other vampires stay? Where was Uncle Vile?"

"Staying was forbidden. I did it for your mother. And I did it secretly. Forty Earth years really isn't that long back home, so your Uncle Vile agreed to cover for me."

"How?"

"He told everyone that I was on a vacation in another galaxy." His father frowned. "Of course, when I returned with a baby, it was a little difficult to explain."

Kevan giggled.

The seriousness quickly returned to his father's face. "That is why I owe so much to your uncle. I am his brother. He protected me—and you. And so I forever owe him my loyalty."

Knowing more about his father's background and his connection to Earth's past, Kevan sympathized with his father's unwavering loyalty to an uncle Kevan believed didn't care for him very much. His Uncle Vile rarely spoke to him, unless he was being ordered about, told to clean a car part, or to bring him a certain type of bolt or tool. But now Kevan understood why his father went along with every one of his uncle's overly ambitious plans—he felt that he owed it to him.

There was a beep and then a crackling sound in the other room that caused Kevan's father to jump abruptly to his feet. He rushed toward Kevan's bedroom door. "It's probably Vile!"

Kevan followed his father, running his fingers through his messy hair and feeling the hunger pangs he often felt after a long nap. He watched as his father raced to answer the call on his video phone. There was a twelve-inch screen mounted to the wall facing the kitchen area that blinked a bright blue light before it was quickly replaced with the image of a face, the sharp-chinned face of his uncle.

"Shawn," Vile barked. "Listen to me. I need your help."

Out of respect for their privacy, Kevan decided to remain quiet and to avoid being seen on the video phone's camera. He tiptoed along the edge of the living room and into the kitchen.

"Yes, Vile," Shawn replied. "Whatever you need."

"I need you to turn up the strength of the psi-shield."

Shawn's face froze. "But why? It's already on such a strong setting."

"Don't question me, Shawn."

Shawn instantly remembered his place and nodded in agreement.

"The ghost woman has powerful connections. I don't want anyone trying to locate her. I can't risk anything getting in the way of tonight's test."

"Yes, brother. I understand."

Kevan rubbed his eyes and wondered about the time. He wasn't sure how long he'd slept, but it couldn't have been for very long. The story his father told him about Earth's past had been intense, causing his head to feel cluttered and sleepy ... *wait ... ghost woman?* He held his breath and waited for his uncle to speak again.

"I have her and those two girls out of the way," Kevan heard his uncle say. He couldn't react; he didn't want his father to see anything in his face that might raise any suspicion. He knew exactly what two girls his uncle was referring to, because he was pretty sure that most teenaged Earth girls didn't associate with ghosts the way they did. Kevan stepped cautiously to the other side of the kitchen to get a better view of the living room. He needed to confirm that his backpack was still on the floor where he'd left it next to the couch. It was.

"I'll adjust the psi-beam's strength immediately," Kevan's father said into the video phone's camera. "Everything will be ready for tonight. We'll meet you at the drive-in just after sun down."

"That's in exactly two hours," Vile confirmed. "Be on time."

"You have the film?"

"Yes, I have the film," Vilester hissed. "Don't worry about what I'm doing. Turn up the beam so the ghost woman can't ruin my plans. And be sure to meet me on Earth just after the sun sets. I want to have everything ready before people start arriving at the drive-in." Vile paused, and if Kevan could have seen the smug look on his uncle's face, he would have been horrified. "Ms. Preston is fading away. Her energy is rapidly depleting. You know what this means, brother?"

"No, Vile, I don't."

He smiled. "It means that very soon, Marilyn Preston will not exist at all."

# Chapter 19

There was an eeriness about Alicia's house that made Kathy's stomach turn. All the curtains were drawn, and they were surrounded in silence. The girls felt helpless. Sir Ghoulingheart had successfully checked them out of school so he could imprison them in Alicia's home under Alicia's father's care. But Alicia's father only stared blankly at the wall, like he wasn't there — the look on his face, chilling Kathy to the bone. And she couldn't imagine what the change in Harold Chavez was doing to her best friend in the entire world — Alicia Chavez.

Knowing how un-Harold-like Harold had become, Kathy risked it and waved her hand at Alicia to get her attention. "Pssst," she said quietly.

Alicia's body jolted. She and Kathy had been sitting quietly at the dining room table, just as Sir Ghoulingheart had instructed them to do before he barked some orders at Harold, took Harold's little red car, and left. Alicia glanced at her father, and just as she expected, he still appeared very interested in something on the wall that no one else could see. She then turned to Kathy.

Kathy tilted her head toward the stairs. "I need to check on Marilyn," she whispered. "I'm worried. I think she's upstairs."

Alicia looked at her father again. He was too dazed-out to notice the girls' conversation. Feeling hopeless, she shrugged her shoulders at Kathy. "What do we do?"

Kathy pointed at Alicia's dad. "What's his favorite thing?"

Alicia squinted her eyes. "What?"

"His favorite thing? Ice cream ... chocolate ... a movie?"

"He likes movies with some stooge guys in them."

"You have them on DVD?" Kathy asked.

Alicia studied her father, disturbed by the emptiness in his face, the lack of sparkle in his eyes. "Yeah, they're on the shelf by the TV. Why?"

Kathy folded her hands and straightened her posture. "Hey, Mr. Chavez?"

There was concern in Alicia's eyes. She desperately and discreetly shook her head no at

Kathy.

But as you probably already guessed, Kathy ignored her. "It's boring just sitting here like this, Mr. Chavez. And I was thinking —"

And as if in a deep trance, Harold responded, "Sir Ghoulingheart, the High Exalted One of Vashmirain, told me to sit here and make sure you two don't do *anything*."

"Well, can we watch a movie?" Kathy asked anyway. "That's not really *doing* anything. It's just … watching."

Harold looked a little puzzled. The question caught him off guard.

So Kathy continued. "Like, maybe a comedy? I happen to like movies about three guys who go on pointless adventures and hit and slap each other a lot. Do you happen to have any movies like that?"

Alicia held her breath, certain the plan wouldn't work. It was too ridiculous.

But surprisingly, Harold's face flickered with interest. "I like movies like that, too!"

"Of course you do," Kathy smiled, quite proud of herself. "That's because you have great taste, Mr. Chavez. I know this about you. I can see it."

He stood, still not making any eye contact with either girl seated in front of him at the table. His gaze still spacey, still unfocused. "I like funny things." His boring, monotone voice was beginning to show a little emotion.

Kathy nodded enthusiastically as she slowly rose from her seat. "Maybe we should watch some TV, Mr. Chavez. Or Ally could look through some DVDs with you and find a funny movie we can all watch. How does that sound?"

Mr. Chavez pointed at a neatly organized collection of movies on a shelf near the fireplace. There was a fresh, child-like glimmer in his eyes.

"Perfect," Kathy said before turning back to Alicia. "You should go help your dad pick out a movie while I go use the bathroom upstairs."

Alicia couldn't believe Kathy's plan was working. She waited anxiously for her father to say something, for him to speak up and stop Kathy from leaving his sight—but he didn't. Instead, he only smiled and headed straight for his movie collection.

Kathy successfully snuck away, taking the stairs to the second floor. Marilyn was up there somewhere. Kathy knew this because she had watched as Sir Ghoulingheart stormed up there to yell about something before dramatically leaving the Chavez home. And while he was up there, they could hear that awful baritone laugh and then a door slam just after he said the words, " ...

or you'll never see daylight again!"

Kathy knew that Marilyn had to be locked inside one of the bedrooms. She was not only determined to find her, but she was also ready to help plan Marilyn's escape. There was something strange about the confidence in Sir Ghoulingheart's evil voice before he'd left the house, and Kathy had plenty of time to think about it in the hours after she and Alicia were left in Mr. Chavez's care. Well, *care* might not be the most appropriate word, actually. Being watched by Mr. Chavez, in his current absent-headed state, was a lot like being watched by one of those little suit-wearing monkeys from the circus. He stared at the walls a lot and scratched his head … sometimes he twitched. In fact, a monkey might have been more fun.

Kathy carefully approached the only room with a closed door — Alicia's room — and reached out for the door knob to turn it as quietly as possible. It was locked. Kathy knelt down and placed her lips close to the crack between the door and its frame. "Aunt Marilyn?" she whispered. "Are you in there?"

Within seconds, a tiny voice answered back, "Yes." The voice was weak and tired.

"Why can't you come through the door?"

"Ghoulingheart is draining my energy," she struggled to say. "I'm cut off ... from the rest of the universe. And without that connection, I will fade away."

Kathy had to remain calm. "But how? How is he doing this?"

Marilyn edged up closer to the door. "There's a powerful shield over this house. It's ... cutting off all energy exchanges on the particle level. Very difficult to explain. The shield is being transmitted down from his ship."

"Oh no."

"You have to escape. You have to stop him from showing that film."

Kathy's eyes began to water. "I can't leave you here. Don't ask me to do something like that. *Please*."

"Kathy," Marilyn continued, drawing up as much strength as she could. "I can't get out. Ghoulingheart is planning to test this film out on your school. It's part of a bigger plan."

Kathy had to steady her breathing, she had to come up with something. She tightened her eyes in frustration. "Isn't there a computer, or a TV, or anything in there that you can get some energy from?" A tear escaped her. "Then you could unlock the door or just walk through it—"

"No, Kathy. I'm not strong enough to pull the energy out of anything." Marilyn's voice was beginning to sound more faded and bits of static could be heard in it as she spoke. "Go back downstairs ... get Alicia ... leave this house."

"But Ghoulingheart said he would hurt you if we tried to leave!"

"I'm already hurt, Kathy," she answered. "Go. Ally's dad won't stop you. Ghoulingheart made a big mistake ... he forgot that he can't control Harold with the psi-shield in place."

Kathy was stunned. "What?!"

"He's using mind control. His thoughts can't get through the shield."

And then Kathy realized that she and Alicia had been sitting around with Harold for almost two full boring hours—completely uncontrolled by him. It was time to collect her thoughts, to be strong, and to prepare herself to do things that she might not want to do—like leaving Marilyn behind. "Okay, I'll get Ally and maybe we'll flag down a city bus, or maybe she has some bikes in her garage or—"

An intense, static-like sound overpowered the entire house, gently rocking and shaking it, causing Kathy to grab ahold of the door frame. It lasted only seconds, but felt strangely abnormal, definitely not something like an earthquake or anything. It was too electrical, too charged ... *was it a lightning strike?* Kathy wondered.

But before she could wonder about it for very long, the sound of things moving about in Alicia's room surprised her. And from under the door, within the light, she could see a shadow.

"Marilyn?" Kathy asked.

A ghostly arm with very pretty nails poked through the door.

Kathy jumped to her feet. "Marilyn!"

The rest of Marilyn stepped effortlessly through the door. She wiggled her hips in excitement, and her face glowed with a most glorious smile. "I feel amazing!"

"What happened?!"

"The psi-shield must have been deactivated," Marilyn explained, still in a state of disbelief. "But you know what this means, don't you, dear?"

Kathy shook her head no.

"It means we have to get out of here and away from Harold. Without the shield, Ghoulingheart can control him again."

Downstairs, it seemed that Harold was having a lot of trouble picking out a movie. As patient as

Alicia was trying to be, she was, in reality, far beyond aggravated by it. She had movies lined up on the floor in front of them — movies that she couldn't stand — and was waiting on her father's decision.

"Dad. You have seen every one of these movies about fifteen times each. It really doesn't matter which one you pick, because they are all ..." Alicia hesitated, forcing herself to swallow back what she had intended to say, "... uh, very good movies with well thought out storylines. You have really good taste. Just pick a movie. Please."

Kathy ran down the stairs and exploded into the living room. "HEY!"

Alicia turned and stared at Kathy with her mouth open. "Yes?"

Kathy was frazzled and out of breath. "Did you feel that boom-thing that just happened?"

"Yeah, I guess so," Alicia replied. "I thought it was one of those electricity mistake things. Like when the lights go out on the whole street."

"IT WASN'T!"

"Okay."

Kathy waved her hands in excitement. "Come on! We have to go!"

"What?" Alicia asked, glancing back at her father.

"COME ON!" Kathy's eyes bulged and darted from wall to ceiling.

Then without warning, Marilyn materialized next to Kathy, grinning from ear to ear. "Sorry to be in such a hurry, Ally. But I need to get out of here as quickly as possible. I think we all should."

Kathy attempted to grab on to Marilyn's arm, but her hand went right through it. She tried to push Marilyn toward the door, but her hands went through her again. "You have to get out now! Go ahead and go! Ally and I will be out in a minute!"

Marilyn nodded and waved at Harold before disappearing. He didn't see Marilyn, and was trying to figure out what the girls were talking about. "Come on where?" Harold asked them. "You girls can't leave. The vampire guy told me to keep an eye on you. Of course, I don't know where he went or when he'll be back, and I think he stole my car ... but he's an important client." He pointed at Kathy. "An important client of *your* father's."

"My father didn't know Sir Ghoulingheart had plans to destroy the world! He gave my dad a fake name, *and* he's a vampire!"

Harold creased his brow. "I'm going to text him."

"Text who?" Alicia asked, remembering that Jimmy had taken her father's phone.

"I'm going to text Sir Ghoulingheart. He told me to let him know if there was any trouble, especially trouble from you, Kathy Preston!" Harold then proceeded to turn about in circles, walking around aimlessly with his arms out, ready to snatch up his phone from someplace ... if he could find it.

Alicia stepped backward, nudged Kathy with her elbow, and then looked at the front door. Kathy took the hint, and the two of them made their way toward it.

Harold was a lost cause. Well, not permanently. As the girls made their way out of the house, he was still inside spinning around in a circle like a dog seeking to bite its own tail. But the girls were pretty sure that he'd become dizzy and give up at some point. Alicia had to tell herself that whatever was wrong with him was temporary, and that it wouldn't be wrong to leave him alone in the house. After all, he was a grown-up—even if his brain was being controlled by a grumpy vampire from outer space.

# Chapter 20

Kevan carefully stepped out of the ship's main control room, gripping the straps of his backpack in his hand, and looked both ways down the hall. What he did—going against his uncle's plans, turning off the psi-shield instead of turning it up as he'd volunteered to do, as he had been entrusted by his father to do—was strictly forbidden. Even though he wasn't officially a part of the ship's crew, he was the son and nephew of vampires who were. Quite important vampires. And he'd gone against their orders. His Uncle Vilester was well respected ... no, *feared* in many galaxies. No one ever dared to go against his commands. But Kevan didn't give it a second thought. Upon hearing his uncle's request, he immediately volunteered to turn up the psi-shield himself, with no intention of actually doing so.

Vilester himself, standing before many of his

peers at a very important meeting before they'd set a course for Earth, made the case for an overall improvement of the vampire image. The universe had the wrong impression when it came to vampires. Vampires needed to be seen as a bit softer, he'd said. A bit less bitey. A little more kind. A lot less creepy-crawly. They needed to be respected for their automotive talents, and that couldn't happen without some sort of a serious image overhaul. With traditions changing and the goals of the vampire community shifting into a different direction, the level of scariness just had to be toned down a bit. Their people needed to move forward, to progress. But the novelty and popularity of Earth's movies were getting in the way.

And that's where Kevan had been left out of things. Before they'd left Vashmirain, he was never let in on the details of the mission. He'd heard his uncle present a grand speech at some fancy meeting. He remembered having to dress up nicely for the event. His uncle—dressed in the absolute finest of Vashmirian threads—was the guest speaker, standing on a stage before hundreds of other vampires in attendance. Kevan remembered how glorious the sound of applause had been, filling the room with such intense energy. But he didn't understand what was going on … or anything about the mission at all … not until his father had filled him in on the origin of Earth's vampire mythology earlier that evening. Then, it all made perfect sense. But were they really on a peaceful mission? Vilester hadn't contacted The Mystical Order of Ghosts, Enigmas, and Cryptids for help. And the use of psi-shields didn't sound very peaceful. He had a lot of questions forming inside his head. And until he could get them answered, that psi-shield had to be shut off—just in case his new friends on Earth were being affected or hurt by it.

And now that he had turned off the shield, there was guilt inside his chest. A guilt that stung. He continued down the long hall, his head filled with thoughts of Kathy and Alicia, and words of encouragement from Kathy's kind Aunt Marilyn. He pushed the guilt away. He had to get off the ship. He had to tell the girls what he'd learned from his father. Together, they would figure it out. And they had to do this before it was too late and before Vilester could do whatever it was that he was trying to do to the people of Earth with his strange, low-budget B-movie.

# Chapter 21

"We need to figure out how to get to the drive-in," Alicia said. She, Kathy, and Marilyn were only blocks away from Alicia's house, sitting on the swings at the neighborhood park.

"School's out by now," Kathy remembered out loud. "Who else do we know that's going to movie night?"

Alicia kicked at a rock beneath her swing. "Lots of kids are going. Beth said she was going for sure. I talked to her about it yesterday. She said her dad's in that car club that helped get the old drive-in ready for tonight. The Pinheads ... no, The Piranhas."

"Call her!" Kathy exclaimed with excitement. "She lives nearby doesn't she? Ask her if she can pick us up!"

"Okay, I will!" Alicia said, her phone already in her hands.

"Wait a minute," Marilyn began, "Where's your little brother, Ally? And your mom? Shouldn't they have been home by now?"

"Oh no," Alicia realized and checked the time on her phone. "It's almost six. Jimmy and my mom should have been home by five."

Marilyn clicked her tongue and shook her head. "I'm a little concerned about your mother and your little brother going home to Harold any time soon." She looked at Alicia with concern in her eyes. "I think you should call her."

"Okay, okay," Kathy jumped out of her swing. "You call your mom and I'll call Bethany. Keep your mom from going to the house. Tell her to go to the store ... to get us some snacks for the movie or something—"

"But there're going to have concession stands at the movie to help raise money for student council!"

"Ally!" Kathy shouted. "We're trying to distract her!"

"Oh yeah," Alicia remembered. "Good point."

"Jimmy's a picky eater, right?"

"Yeah. The whole city knows that."

Kathy pointed a finger into the air as an excellent idea struck. "Tell your mom to stop at the store to get Jimmy something to eat during the movie. I mean, all they're going to sell at the drive-in tonight are hotdog, chips, and all that other stuff he hates."

"Yes! What a great idea!"

"You call your mom, get her to avoid your house, and I'll call Bethany to see if she can pick us up on their way to the drive-in."

Marilyn smiled. "Good plan, girls. And I'll stay here with you until Bethany arrives. And as soon as I know you're both safe and on your way to the drive-in, I'll pop on over there ahead of you."

"Perfect!" Kathy said. "Wait! No! What if Ghoulingheart is there? He can see you even when you're invisible, can't he?"

Marilyn sighed. "Yes, he can. I'll just have to be as careful as possible. Don't worry about me. I'll keep my distance until I figure something out." She paused to think. "Maybe I can get Jonathan to go with me."

"Yeah," Kathy agreed. "I think it would be better if you were there with Mr. Walsh. I don't think you should go alone."

Alicia had her phone to her ear. "Mom? Where are you?"

Kathy and Marilyn stopped to listen.

"Uh huh ... okay ... so Jimmy's with you?" Alicia nodded. "Okay good. Listen mom, you can't go to the house. Dad made me promise not to tell you, but … he's planning something special for you for after the movie."

Kathy covered her mouth to hold in the laughter.

"He bought flowers and stuff—oops! I wasn't supposed to tell you!" Alicia cringed, feeling terrible for lying. "Maybe you can get Jimmy something to eat on the way to the movie. I know you're not supposed to bring in any outside food, but he needs to eat something … and you can't go home yet!"

Kathy had an idea. "Tell her there's a special on pizza this week at Goobers Pizzeria!"

Alicia pulled the phone away from her face. "How's she gonna sneak a whole pizza into the drive-in?!"

"It's a drive-in! She can drive it in with her car!"

"Girls!" Marilyn hissed. She pointed at the phone in Kathy's hands. "Kathy, you should be calling Bethany. Let's stay focused."

"Right," Kathy calmly agreed. She scrolled through the list of contacts on her phone while quietly singing to herself, "Goobers Goobers, it's terrific. Drive over fast, but don't get a speeding ticket. Pepperoni, olives, jalapenos, and cheese. And the extra parmesan is always free!"

When Bethany's dad pulled up to the drive-in, there were hardly any other cars around. Alicia and Kathy scanned the parking area, looking for anything amiss, anything that wasn't right. The place was already quite spooky and unusual-looking: a bleak, dusty dirt parking area that faced a large blank projection screen, a rather plain brick building toward the back, and all of it surrounded by groups of old, gloomy trees, some still holding onto their leaves and some without.

Bethany's dad parked his old car next to another old car just outside the parking area. "Old" wasn't what Bethany's dad called his car — he used the word "classic" instead. Earlier, when he'd pulled up to the park, Kathy asked him what type of old car it was that he was driving. Stylish and sleek, it did have a pretty intense coolness factor about it. The bubbly curves, deep purple paint job, and its low proximity to the road, made it look like it was floating as it approached. And that super cool rumble ... Bethany's dad was sure proud of that.

"It's a 1940 coupe," Bethany's dad answered. "You like it?"

"Yeah." Kathy smiled. "It's pretty cool."

"Oh no," Bethany said. "Don't start talking

about cars, Dad. It's embarrassing."

"How's it embarrassing?" her father asked with a youthful grin on his face. His slicked-back hair glistened in the sunset that was shining through the car's perfectly clean windows. "Is your dad into cars, Kathy?"

"No. He's into pie charts and profits."

Bethany's father laughed. "How about your dad, Alicia?"

Alicia squirmed in her seat. "His car is ... regular."

"Oh. Well, that's okay."

And after he parked next to the other old car at the drive-in, he removed his seatbelt and turned to the girls. "I'm just going to run over to the projection booth back there." Then he pointed at the building toward the back. "You see it?"

All three girls nodded.

Bethany did a quick scan of their surroundings. "Dad, it's creepy out here."

"You can get out of the car and walk around. Just stick together and stay within viewing distance. I'll be able to see you from inside the booth. See the windows? I'll only be a minute or two anyway. Just seeing if Joe needs anything before he gets started. He's going to be stuck in there during the entire movie, running the projector."

"Okay, Dad," Bethany replied.

Her father exited the car, and the three girls looked at each other in silence for a few moments until Alicia cleared her throat. "Wanna get out and walk around?"

"It's kinda chilly out," Bethany said.

Alicia playfully pushed on the back of Bethany's seat. "Come on. Let's get out and look around," she said, looking at Kathy for help.

"Yeah, Beth," Kathy chimed in. "Let's get out and walk around. It's cramped back here in your dad's old car."

"Okay, okay," Bethany said. She opened her door and stepped out. She pulled her seat up so Alicia and Kathy could climb out from the back.

But as soon as Alicia and Kathy got out, they both gawked at Bethany with surprised looks on their faces.

"What?" Bethany asked.

"You're dressed like the 1950s!" Alicia cried out, pointing at Bethany's poofy blue poodle skirt.

"Well, yeah," Bethany said. "That's the theme of the night. I heard that kid Randy's coming dressed as a cheesy alien, which isn't really 1950s, but at least it goes with the whole science fiction movie-thing, I guess."

Alicia turned to Kathy in a panic. "We forgot about our outfits!"

"I'm already on it." She was texting as fast as she could into her phone. "My dad's going to have to bring them."

"Mine too?"

"Of course, Ally." She smiled. "With your dad being all weird and crazy, I took care of it for you."

Alicia had to look away, embarrassed and thankful at the same time.

"Now," Kathy began as she slipped her phone back into her jacket, "let's keep an eye out for Marilyn. She should be around here somewhere with Mr. Walsh."

Bethany had a perplexed look on her face. "The English teacher?"

"Maybe she's in that building Beth's dad went into!" Alicia suggested.

"Hmmm. Maybe."

Then Bethany asked, "Who's Marilyn?"

"She's Kathy's aunt," Alicia answered.

"Yeah," Kathy answered. "No big deal."

"Oh. Well, ... is that her car?" Bethany pointed behind them, into a group of trees.

Both girls spun around to see an older black car in the distance.

"No," Kathy answered robotically. "She doesn't drive ... anymore." She quickly turned to Alicia. "What does Mr. Walsh drive? A green something, right?"

"Oh," Bethany began, "Maybe it's another one of my dad's friends. I know it's not Mr. Joe's car. His is that gray one over there by the projection building."

Alicia frowned and looked over at the building toward the back. "Didn't your dad say he'd only be a minute?"

"I guess so," Bethany answered. "Maybe they got caught up in a conversation. You haven't been around these guys like I have. They talk a lot about man stuff."

Kathy studied Alicia's face with a most curious expression. She pursed her lips and narrowed her eyes until they were wrinkled around the edges.

"What?" Alicia asked her.

"Let's go over there and see what the holdup is."

"What for?" Alicia asked nervously. "Shouldn't we be waiting around for your dad? Or for Mr. Walsh and Marilyn?"

"I have an idea whose car that is in those trees over there." Kathy seemed pretty confident about it, too. She lifted her head into the air and nodded assuredly.

But it didn't make sense to Alicia. "Sir Ghoulingheart? But he took my dad's car."

"So? He's a magical space vampire. I'm sure he can change the car into whatever he wants it to be. Or maybe he stole another car on the way over."

Bethany glanced over her shoulders and took a few cautious steps away from them. "Wait. Magical space vampire? What's going on?"

Kathy grabbed a hold of Alicia's arm. "He could be in that projection room with Beth's dad and his friend Joe!"

"*What*?!" Bethany cried out. "But there's no such thing as vampires! That car over there probably belongs to one of my dad's other friends!"

"It's hidden in the trees, Beth. Car guys want their cars to be seen, not hidden," Kathy said with confidence. "Come on, you guys. Let's go over to the projection room and see what's going on!"

The girls stared at each other for a few seconds. Alicia smiled at Bethany, worried about what she might learn about the whole vampire situation, hoping that she could handle it. Kathy certainly didn't seem too concerned about dragging Bethany into the middle of things. But Kathy also knew that time was against them, so whatever strange things Bethany might learn or was about to see, there was nothing they could do to prevent it.

"Alright," Bethany said. "Let's go."

On the outside, the projection booth was made of brick that had been painted white. The girls were careful to walk softly as they made their approach. The closer they got to the small building, the more cautious they had to be. There were a few windows facing them, and a few large film projectors could be seen through the glass.

Kathy motioned with her hands that they should all duck down a bit. She then pointed at the side of the building. Muffled voices could be heard inside.

"Come on," Kathy whispered.

And on the side of the building, with their backs to the wall, the three girls could hear the conversation going on inside. Luckily, or perhaps unluckily for them, someone had left the back door open. Otherwise, it would have been very difficult to hear anything going on inside since the projection booth was made to be soundproof.

"… and I will ask you one last time to tell me exactly when the rest of your car club is expected to arrive."

Kathy and Alicia looked at each other in terror. The voice very distinctly, and disgustingly, belonged to Sir Ghoulingheart.

"And I already told you, man! I'm not telling you a single thing!" Another voice said.

"Ah ... well, I will just have to tie you up, or put you into a deep sleep like your friend over there in the corner," Sir Ghoulingheart threatened. "I was trying to play nicey nice with you, human, since I really like your 1940s coupe. The flake on that purple paint job is quite perfect."

"NO!" Bethany yelled.

Both Kathy and Alicia were taken by surprise to see Bethany rush toward the back door, her fists clenched tightly in front of her. Kathy immediately pulled on Bethany's skirt as she ran past, trying to stop her. But it was too late. In an instant, Ghoulingheart was standing at the open door in a long black cape, staring, and smiling the wickedest smile at them, causing Bethany to lose her courage.

"Hello, girls," he said to them. He strolled over and crossed his arms. And if you could imagine for a second, the most intimidating look that any face was capable of ... he had it.

Bethany shrank down and moved in as close as possible to her friends.

Sir Ghoulingheart crouched down, getting close to Bethany's face. "You are the daughter of the man with the purple coupe. Do you want to know how I know this?"

Bethany only trembled in response.

"I know this because your father has been thinking of you and your safety as I have been questioning him. I saw your face inside his cluttered mind."

"Leave her alone!" Alicia's voice shook as she spoke.

"All of you," Sir Ghoulingheart roared, paralyzing the three of them with fear, "are coming with me. And you," he said to Bethany, "… you will tell me exactly when the rest of your father's friends will arrive … in their nice, detailed, rebuilt automobiles."

# Chapter 22

Kevan stared into his bedroom mirror and adjusted the leather jacket he had on over his favorite black T-shirt. He'd fixed his hair into the perfect Earth-retro pompadour, exactly the way he'd seen in several photos. There was no time to second guess his plan. And as far as he knew, no one had figured out that the psi-shield aimed at Alicia's house had been turned off.

Overhead, an electrical pop sound caught his attention. It was coming from the ship's speaker system.

"*Attention,*" said a voice in a serious tone. It was his father, Shawn. "*All drivers included in tonight's test mission must prepare for immediate departure. Our orders have been received, and coordinates are set. I repeat, drivers must prepare for departure. It is confirmed to be ten drivers. Other drivers will remain on standby, on my orders, until further notice.*"

Kevan inhaled a deep breath before turning to

grab his backpack from the bed. He had to get back to Kathy and Alicia. He just had to tell them what he'd learned from his father. And if he couldn't convince his father to let him go with him to the drive-in, he was going to have to sneak his way in.

The girls sat nervously inside the projection booth with their hands tied behind their backs. Sir Ghoulingheart had turned the lights out and said a few menacing things to them before leaving, warning them against trying to escape because he would do something to Bethany's dad if they did. Of course, all the while, Kathy fidgeted with the rope around her wrists, envisioning what escape artist Harry Houdini might have done in the same situation. Then, Sir Ghoulingheart took Bethany's dad along with him, pulling him through the door by the collar of his bowling-style shirt. Bethany cried until Alicia was able to calm her down, and the projectionist named Joe that Bethany's dad wanted to visit was snoring away in the corner next to a bunch of old film equipment. Kathy guessed that Sir Ghoulingheart had callously used a sleeping spell or some sort of powerful hypnosis on the poor man. Either way, he was in such a deep sleep, that Sir Ghoulingheart hadn't even bothered to tie him up.

Bethany wasn't easy to console. Because her father had been strong enough to block his thoughts, not to give up the location of his car club, Ghoulingheart had quickly turned his attention to Bethany instead. And as soon as he flashed his fangs at her, Bethany caved. She told him that, to avoid traffic, The Piranhas would be taking a back road on their way to the theater. She didn't remember the name of the road, but that didn't matter. Sir Ghoulingheart gazed deeply into her thoughts, and when he did, he could hear a conversation her father had on the phone earlier that evening, giving him every detail he needed to know.

"It's not your fault, Beth," Alicia said for the tenth time. "You didn't know he could read your mind."

Bethany's face was set into the saddest look the girls had ever seen her make. "But vampires aren't real. It's just a costume, right?"

"Sorry, Beth," Kathy said while still struggling with the rope. "They're real and they read minds. Especially weak minds."

"Hey!" Bethany said angrily in between sobs. "Are you saying I have a weak mind?!"

"Sorry," Kathy answered in frustration, "I

didn't mean it like that. You didn't know how powerful his mind was when you let him see right through you like that. At least your dad knew how to keep his thoughts private."

"Kathy!" Alicia scooted in closer to Bethany for a show of support. "Beth didn't know vampires could read minds. You're not being fair."

"Correction," Kathy added with heavy sarcasm, "vampires from outer space. Sir Ghoulingheart is probably, like, a thousand years old. He probably has one of the most powerful mind-reading brains in the universe."

"What's going on here?!" Bethany asked in pure panic. "This isn't really happening, is it?! So a vampire ... a *real* vampire, took my dad?!"

"Space vampire," Kathy added quietly.

"It's okay, Beth," Alicia told her. "He messed with my dad, too."

A gentle sizzling sound above the girls' heads caught their attention. The girls looked up to see the face of a rather beautiful ghost poking through the ceiling, upside down—it was Marilyn. Her dark-brown hair hung down all over the place, making her look very silly as she flashed a huge smile at them. "Hi, girls!"

"Marilyn!" Kathy beamed with delight. "I'm so glad you're here! We're tied up!"

"Not anymore!" she replied.

The ropes instantly disintegrated and the girls' hands were free. Marilyn pulled the rest of her ghostly body through the ceiling, performed a mid-air somersault, and landed on her feet in front of them. She was dressed in a light pink 1950s cardigan and a pair of shapely black slacks. "Cars are beginning to arrive. We need to —"

The sharp and sudden sound of a snore interrupted her.

Marilyn spun around to see a man curled up in the corner behind her. "Who's that?"

"I think he's the projectionist," Alicia answered. "His name's Joe. Ghoulingheart did that to him. He won't wake up."

"Yeah," Kathy added as she got up from the floor, "and he also stacked our cell phones on that table over there and tied us up."

"Oh," Marilyn answered as she shook her head and checked behind her for the cell phones. "Well, cars are starting to arrive. So we need to hurry. Jonathan's waiting in the parking area, trying to blend in." Marilyn stopped speaking and stared straight ahead with great concern at Bethany. And Bethany's red, teary eyes were staring straight back at Marilyn, as wide as they had ever been. "Is she okay?"

"Beth?" Kathy placed a hand on Bethany's shoulder. "Are you all right?"

Alicia patted Bethany on the back. "She just saw a vampire and a ghost for the first time in her entire life. I think she's just a little freaked out. That's all."

"Oh, where are my manners?" Marilyn held out her hand to Bethany. "My name is Marilyn. And yours, I already know, is Bethany. How nice to meet you."

Bethany took a clumsy step closer to Alicia and began to tremble.

"Sorry, Beth," Kathy began. "We don't really have time for you to be scared like this. We'll have to explain things later."

"Hey!" Alicia said while pointing a finger at Marilyn. "She's in 1950s clothing, too!"

"Don't worry, Ally," Kathy tried to remind her. "My dad's probably on his way with our outfits."

Marilyn sighed impatiently. "Listen, I'll go get your outfits and come right back. You'll have to change in the tiny bathroom back there as quickly as you can. Then we seriously need to get back to saving the planet. Okay?"

"Saving it from what?" Bethany was afraid to ask.

"From the space vampires, dear," Marilyn

replied before disappearing.

Kathy started counting on her fingers. "One ... two ... three ..."

"I'm scared," said Bethany.

"... four ... five ..."

And with a bluish-green flash, Marilyn was back, holding two outfits in her hands. "Here," she said in a hurry, handing one of the outfits to Alicia and the other to Kathy.

The girls looked at the clothes in their hands and then at each other in disappointment. "I want the black one," Kathy said to Alicia.

Alicia agreed. "Let's trade."

"Hurry, girls!" Marilyn urged them as they scurried into the bathroom. "People are starting to arrive! Sir Ghoulingheart will be back soon to begin showing his film! We are all in great danger!"

And then Bethany said in a sweet, wimpy little voice, "A vampire took my dad."

Marilyn looked down at her with a sympathetic smile. "I'm sorry, dear. You're not having a very good day, are you?"

She slowly shook her head no.

"It's all right. We're going to stop that naughty vampire. Would you like to help?"

Bethany nodded, looking less afraid than

before.

"Good. Do you happen to know where the vampire went with your father?"

"I don't know," Bethany answered. "The vampire wanted to know what road The Piranhas were going to take to get here. I didn't want to tell him, but he read my mind, and then he left with my dad after he found out."

Marilyn looked very concerned upon hearing this. "That doesn't sound very good."

# Chapter 23

The sun, now well below the horizon, left only a few patches of deep orange and purplish colors in the clouds above where it disappeared to make way for the night. A cool chill was ready to envelop the city of San Antonio. Nothing too windy, nothing too frigid — it was just perfect for a night at the drive-in theater. Unless you were a member of The Piranhas car club. And if members of The Piranhas had known this, they would have turned their classic cars around and headed back to the safety of their homes instead of getting on that dark, empty back road where a group of fiendish vampires were waiting to abduct them.

It only took seconds to accomplish. With the help of a large silver space ship hovering overhead, and a beam of red light to pull the cars up with, it was almost effortless. And as soon as the spaceship flew away with The Piranhas inside, another spaceship took its place; that one containing the exact same amount of cars and drivers that had just been taken from the desolate back road.

The bottom of the second ship opened and a misty blue beam shot down from it, illuminating the road and many of the tall trees nearby. One by one, shiny, elaborately detailed hot rods descended from the ship and landed safely on the road below. Each hot rod containing a confident, grinning vampire driver, complete in 1950s Earth clothing: slick black leather jackets, jeans, poofy skirts, and sleek hairdos. Every one of them looked like they'd come fresh out of a retro Hollywood movie.

As the silver space ship ascended back into the stars, the driver of the first car stepped out and raised his arm into the air. It was Sir Ghoulingheart's faithful brother, Shawn. "Tonight, we are The Piranhas!" he announced loudly so that every vampire in every car lined up on the road could hear him. The vampire drivers cheered in return, as Kevan, who was sitting in the back seat of his father's cherished red 1950s convertible, frowned sadly instead.

"Once we arrive, we will get into the planned

formation, and we will wait for my brother's command before we begin!"

A few of the female drivers pulled out make up compacts to quickly add more white powder to their already pale faces.

Shawn canvassed the trees that swayed in the light wind along the roadside and inhaled a clean, comforting breath. He lifted his chin into the night air and looked over at Kevan with a smile. "I'm glad you wanted to join us tonight, son. We will create a new history on Earth. It's a proud day for our people."

Kevan hid the doubt in his face and allowed himself to nod in return. "Thanks for letting me be a part of it, Dad."

Marilyn peeked her head around the back wall of the projection booth, looking to see if Sir Ghoulingheart was anywhere nearby waiting. All three girls were lined up behind her, carefully scanning the trees for any sign of vampires.

By the time Alicia and Kathy had changed into their movie night outfits, Bethany seemed to have pulled herself together, accepting the fact that they were going to help stop a villainous vampire with the help of a beautiful ghost. Still a little shaken, Bethany was beginning to show a little more of a vigilant side. Her hands were balled into fists again, and she had a determined scowl on her face. Before the girls grabbed their phones and snuck out through the back door of the booth, Bethany had even volunteered to take on Sir Ghoulingheart herself with some moves she had learned in Karate classes. Of course, Marilyn was quick to talk her out of it.

"What's going on out there, Marilyn?" Kathy asked. "Do you see him?"

"Do you see my dad?" Bethany asked eagerly.

"No," Marilyn replied. "But this place sure is filling up fast ... so many cars ... and so many cute outfits!"

"Oooooh! I want to see!" Alicia said with a bubbly voice. "Here, take a picture with my phone!"

Kathy pushed Alicia's phone aside. "Put that thing away! You'll see everything soon enough."

"I just want to make sure no one's wearing the same outfit as me."

Kathy playfully rolled her eyes. "Are you serious? I special ordered these from a boutique in Los Angeles. No one else is going to look as cool as we do. No offense, Beth."

Bethany frowned.

A sudden gasp from Marilyn startled the girls.

"I see a bunch of classic cars pulling into the parking area! It must be The Piranhas!"

"Let me see!" Bethany yelped, pushing through Kathy and Alicia before they had a chance to stop her. She poked her head around the corner, looking right through Marilyn's midsection, and searched the crowded parking area with desperate eyes. "I don't recognize those cars. Those aren't my dad's friends."

"Are you sure?" Marilyn asked.

"I'm positive," Bethany answered. "I see their cars all the time … every Sunday when they meet up. Those cars are different … fancier."

"Fancier?" Kathy asked, pulling Bethany back by the arm. "Let me see."

"Girls!" Marilyn warned as all three girls now struggled to see around the brick wall. "We must be careful not to be seen!"

"Look!" Kathy exclaimed. "It's Kevan!"

"Where?" Alicia asked.

"There!" Kathy pointed at a red convertible to the far right, just outside the main parking area. Inside it sat a boy in a shiny black leather jacket with his hair slicked back.

He looked so different, that Alicia didn't recognize him. "How do you know for sure?"

"Who's Kevan?" Bethany asked.

"He's a boy Kathy likes," Alicia answered.

"I do not!"

"*And* he's a vampire."

"Ally!" Kathy glared at her with strong piercing eyes, which normally would have scared Alicia quite terribly, but there was hardly any time to think about the repercussion of her actions at that moment.

Marilyn turned and pointed a finger at them. "You both need to stop this right away. We have more important things to worry about than crushes on vampire boys. I had a crush once on a half-man half-bigfoot, and he hardly stunk at all, but ... you know what? Never mind about that. Forget I said it."

"Actually, that boy does look kinda cute." Bethany smiled. "From back here."

"Well, we need to get his attention," Marilyn suggested.

"Kathy can text him," Alicia said.

"No," Marilyn replied quickly. "Don't send a text. There's a man standing too close to him, just outside the car. He might be another vampire." She paused. "I'm worried that they're all vampires."

"What do you mean?" Alicia asked.

"The drivers of the old cars," she clarified.

"Bethany doesn't recognize them. I think this is a part of their plan. Something to do with the movie."

Kathy snapped her fingers. "That makes perfect sense!"

Marilyn turned to Bethany with an uneasy smile on her face. "Bethany, do you think you could walk over there and tell that boy Kevan to meet us back here?"

Bethany froze.

Alicia giggled. "Bethany has a hard enough time talking to Earth boys. How's she going to talk to a vampire one?"

But in a dire situation, such as theirs, Bethany was easy to convince. They explained that all she had to do was walk up to the car Kevan was in, politely get his attention without alerting anyone else nearby, and inform him that she was a friend of Kathy's and Alicia's. She would explain that the girls were hiding behind the projection booth with Marilyn, and then ask that he meet with them there to figure out their next move.

Bethany, nervous but pumped up and ready to help, agreed. She walked over to the car as smoothly as her wobbly legs would let her. Frightened, she checked for any sign of vampires along the way. Once she got there, the words she said to Kevan didn't go exactly as planned. But considering that she didn't really have time to plan anything, much less, how to approach and converse with a teenaged vampire, that was okay.

"Uh … hi. Um, my name's Bethany. I'm a friend of Kathy's and, don't bite me, Alicia's. They want to talk to you back there and, don't bite me, there's a lady who's a ghost, too … um, this is all really weird. I like your jacket … don't bite me."

# Chapter 24

Kevan checked his hair, patting and feeling it with his hands, as lightly as possible, while keeping a steady eye on Bethany. He was almost as afraid of her as she was of him. She walked alongside him back to the projection booth, but with a pronounced and exaggerated distance between them, making it look as if she was allergic to him.

Marilyn shook her head and smiled at them as they approached. "Thank you for getting Kevan. That was very brave of you to trust us like that, Bethany."

"Brave of *her*?" Kevan asked.

Bethany's eyes bulged, and she moved farther away from him.

Kathy rushed right into questioning Kevan. "What's going on? Who are the people driving the old cars? I like your outfit, where'd you get it?"

"Uh …" Kevan swallowed, thinking on where

to start. "I have the film here in my bag," he said, pointing to the backpack hanging on his shoulder. "The people driving the cars are vampires. They took the other car club with one of our ships, and we took their place."

They all reacted with stunned looks on their faces, including Kevan because he didn't know what else to do.

"Where's my dad?" Bethany asked.

Kevan didn't understand the question and only looked at Bethany in confusion.

Marilyn explained, "Your uncle tied the girls up and took this girl's father with him just before people started to arrive. Do you know where your uncle went? He has the film with the secret messages on it."

"No," Kevan answered. "I haven't seen him, but listen ..." He paused to think. "I know what's going on tonight, and I don't think it's as bad as we thought it was earlier."

"Kevan," Marilyn began, "we don't have a lot of time. Your uncle put some sort of mind control spell on a man inside this projection booth. I'm sure he plans to return at exactly seven o'clock to put his copy of the film in the projector. That's in only," she waited as Kathy showed her the time on her phone, "five minutes."

"Yes, I know, but—"

"What I need you to do, Kevan, is to hide back here and wait for your uncle to return with the film. Then, somehow, we'll switch it before he can load it into the projector so that whatever he's planning to do, won't work. By the time he figures out it's the wrong film, the girls and I will have the entire city's police force out here surrounding the theater. Which will give me enough time to get The Order's permission to force your uncle to cease his foolish plans or face the penalty of a universal safety violation."

Kevan raised his eyebrows at her in silence.

"You don't think it'll work?"

"No, I don't. And I need to explain something about what's going on before we do anything else."

"We are short on time, Kevan."

An intense mix of sadness and worry filled his eyes. "I think we should let him show the film."

"What?!" both Kathy and Alicia snapped at the same time.

"This is all a huge misunderstanding. I know all of this seems kind of evil … but my uncle is just a dramatic kind of guy, you know? Everything with him ends up becoming big and dramatic like this. It just *looks* evil. He and my dad are just trying to fix things ... to put them back the way they were. That's all. It's a lot to explain, so you're just going to have to trust me, okay?"

"Yes," Sir Ghoulingheart's voice commanded from above their heads. He gently floated down from the roof of the building with his arms crossed in front of him. "You're just going to have to trust us."

Kevan looked into Marilyn's eyes, as if to say sorry, hoping she'd understand.

Sir Ghoulingheart placed a hand on Kevan's shoulder. "I am proud of you, Kevan. Prouder than I have ever been."

"I'm sorry I turned off the psi-shield," he said to his uncle with trembling words. "But I knew if I could just explain to them what was going on tonight, they'd understand and Marilyn wouldn't contact The Order to try and stop you."

"Ah," his uncle said calmly, contemplatively. "I understand, Kevan. At first, I was upset about the psi-shield, but not any longer. Unfortunately though, I do believe that you are too trusting of your friends here. Marilyn has already contacted The Mystical Order," he turned to her, "haven't you?"

She nodded once in return.

"And so now, she is merely waiting for backup

and for permission to step in and stop me. Because, you see, she technically cannot do anything until we have done something *wrong* … which we haven't."

Marilyn stood tall. "You've tied children up, placed a psi-shield over a house, and abducted an entire car club!"

Bethany punched Sir Ghoulingheart on the arm. "And where's my dad, you jerk?!"

"Ow!" Sir Ghoulingheart cried out while brandishing an awkward smile, attempting to mask the pain. "Little girl, your father was useless to me. He knows nothing about operating film projectors, so he is working the hotdog stand. And I have already caught him eating some of them. He also talks with his mouth full."

Alicia could feel her phone receive a text message.

"No, *you* talk with *your* mouth full!" Bethany shot back.

Sir Ghoulingheart sighed. "Little girl, your insults are not carefully thought out."

Alicia sneakily turned to check her phone. It was a text from her little brother Jimmy that read, "I gots pizza. We are here, baby!"

"… and I think I am going to have to put you in the trunk of a car until the film is over. Obviously, tying you girls up didn't work."

Marilyn pulled Bethany away from Sir Ghoulingheart and shielded her with transparent arms. "You're not doing anything to her at all!"

Sir Ghoulingheart smirked, but remained silent, curious to hear more from Marilyn.

She pointed a nervous, defiant finger at him. "You're going to go inside that projection booth, and you're going to wake up that poor man sleeping in the corner, and let him show the film he's supposed to show to these families tonight."

"Kevan," Sir Ghoulingheart said with an amused smile, "I want you to help make sure that these girls do nothing to ruin my plans. Do you understand?"

Kevan looked to the ground. "Yes, sir."

Ghoulingheart then stepped in closer to Marilyn, intimidating her with his cold, wretched stare. "And I will take care of you myself, Ms. Preston."

# Chapter 25

"How could you do this to us, Kevan?!" Kathy hissed. She, Alicia, and Kevan were walking toward his father's convertible.

"I tried to explain everything, but nobody's listening to me."

"Look what your uncle is doing," Alicia pointed out. "Do you think locking your friends inside car trunks is normal?"

Kevan thought about it, knew that it wasn't normal, but pretended that in some way, somewhere, perhaps it could be a normal sort of thing to do to your friends. Maybe.

"And look what he's doing to Marilyn and Bethany!" Kathy reminded him with a sharp tongue. "You heard what he said. He threatened to hurt them if we didn't go along with all of this!" Not seeing any reaction from Kevan, Kathy's face grew more furious, and she slowed her pace toward the car. "And now he's got them trapped in that projection booth with him!"

Kevan's father saw them approaching and got out of the front seat of his car to confront his son. "Excuse me, Kevan," he said with a snarl on his lips and a cautious eye. "Who are these ... people?"

"Um ... well, Uncle Vilester told me to put them in the trunk of your car."

"*Both* of them? I'm not sure they'll fit."

Kathy was quite offended by the callousness of this reaction, because a part of her had expected this man to be very shocked and disturbed at the idea of locking two girls inside of a car's trunk. And for a split second, she thought he might actually grab them by the wrists and lead them off to safety. But he didn't. And this upset Kathy very much.

"This is crazy!" Kathy announced.

Kevan's father studied the back of his car. "I think we can only get one in there. We'll put the other one in Fred's car."

Alicia's mouth dropped open.

Kevan's father tossed him his car keys and said, "Glad you're helping your uncle, son. I'm proud of you. I'll go talk to Fred." Then he walked away.

Kevan gazed at the keys in his hand, and then moved in closer to the back of his father's car.

"Come on. One of you has to get in," he said without emotion.

Kathy walked up to the car and stood beside Kevan. "I'll get in after you tell me why you changed your mind about helping them instead of us."

Kevan didn't see the harm in that. Telling her a little about his people's history and why the people of Earth had to be ... *had* to be ... brainwashed ... wait, *brainwashed*? And then Kevan realized something that troubled him—he had no idea what his uncle's plan really was, or how hidden messages in a movie were supposed to help solve anything. It was one simple drive-in theater with only sixty cars parked inside the parking area. The rest of the cars, staggered along the perimeter, belonged to his uncle's car club. "I don't know."

Kathy looked puzzled. "What do you mean?"

Kevan tossed his backpack into the back seat of the car. "My dad started telling me about a mistake our people made when they visited Earth hundreds and hundreds of years ago," Kevan began with a distant, glazed look in his eyes, "but what I really don't understand is how a mistake that big can be fixed in one night at a movie theater like this one."

Kathy could see how much Kevan was second guessing himself. She waved at Alicia to move in closer while she thought of what to ask him next. "Did your father tell you their plan?"

"No."

"So what was this big mistake your people made on Earth?"

Kevan hesitated. "They were seen by humans. I guess they weren't being careful. The humans were afraid of what they saw. The vampires had to make them feel safe again."

"How?" asked Alicia.

"They made up stories about our weaknesses," Kevan replied. "They told them lies so they'd feel safe again ... so they'd come out of their homes and go back to living normal lives. But those stories became legends. Legends that hurt and labeled our people."

"Oh my goodness, Kevan," Kathy said in astonishment. "What parts were made up? What did your people tell them?"

"I don't get it," Alicia said. "They lied about what can hurt vampires?"

"Yes!" Kathy understood completely. "He's saying that whatever we've believed all this time about vampires, isn't true! Right?"

"Right," Kevan confirmed.

Alicia frowned. "I didn't even believe in vampires until a few days ago."

In her excitement, Kathy got a little too close to Kevan's face. "Garlic?"

"Only slightly," he admitted. "Our people have been getting a vaccine for that stuff for thousands of years now."

"Sunlight?"

"The suns in a few solar systems are bothersome, but not the one in yours."

"Crosses?"

"They could. But only if made from the wood of a certain type of tree."

Kathy gasped. "This is incredible! But why? Why would your people care what our people think?"

Kevan answered, "Believe it or not, the Internet of your planet has a wide audience. Your digital uploads can be viewed all over the universe. Vampire movies and documentaries ... digital books and independent films. Earth's vampire movies make it look like we hunt down and attack people on your planet. It's hurting our reputation."

"Wow," Kathy replied. "This is just unbelievable."

"Kathy," Kevan said as he placed the key into

the trunk's lock, "I still need you to get in the trunk."

"*What*?!"

"We need to play along," he explained. "I want to ask around and find out what's really going on. I'll be as quick as I can."

"Fine," she agreed. "But just tell me one more thing."

"Okay, what?"

"What *does* hurt you guys? If it's not garlic anymore, it has to be something."

Kevan didn't know how to answer. It was forbidden to say, but he wanted her to trust him. And more than anything, he just wanted to be valued by someone, to be considered useful. So he decided to tell her. "Parmesan cheese."

"You're joking, right?"

"No. The stuff's aged, weird, it's powdery, and smells funny. If someone throws it in your face, you can breathe it in, and it makes you feel like you're on fire." Kevan opened the trunk and pointed inside.

Kathy nodded. "Alright, but promise me that as soon as you find out something bad about your uncle's plan, you'll come back and let me out."

"I promise."

Reluctantly, Kathy climbed into the trunk, one

leg after the other, and connected her worried eyes with Alicia's as Kevan slowly closed the trunk. Feeling ashamed and in more doubt than earlier, he had a difficult time turning to face Alicia.

"I'm next, huh?"

But before he could answer, Kevan's father placed a hand on Kevan's shoulder and said, "Fred says you can put the girl in his trunk, as long as she doesn't scream a lot or anything annoying like that. Human screams irritate him."

"Oh," Kevan replied. "Dad?"

"Yes, son?"

"About tonight … I was wondering … how are we going to fix things, you know, change Earth's opinion about us with one film?" Kevan's lips trembled when asking. "How's one theater going to help change the views of an entire planet?"

His father glanced at Alicia before answering, "This is an experiment, son. We're simply testing this film out on these people tonight." He leaned in close to him. "Now, I think we should get this other girl into Fred's trunk. And don't worry, we'll let the girls out as soon as the film gets to the good parts and we have everything under control. We wouldn't want them to miss it." Shawn Ghoulingheart flashed a frightening grin at Alicia. "Come here, young lady. We are running out of time."

Alicia shuddered, taking a step closer toward them.

"But, Dad?" Kevan continued, "What do you mean, *it's an experiment*? Does that mean it might not work?"

"Well," his father shrugged uneasily while answering, "we're not certain what will happen to the humans' brainwaves after they view the film. That's all."

Kevan couldn't believe what his father said. "What?"

"The messages in the film cannot be seen or heard correctly by the humans without the proper sound frequency tuning. It's very complicated and difficult to explain. It's like they're being re-programmed."

"Can it *hurt* them?"

His father's face contorted slightly. "Maybe."

"Permanently?"

"We'll find out soon enough. That's why it's called a test, son. Now let's get this young lady out of the way so your uncle can start the film."

Kevan stepped in front of Alicia and stood tall. "How's that supposed to fix things? It sounds like it could make things a lot worse!"

"Kevan! I command you to do as you have been

told—"

"It's okay," Alicia interrupted in a delicate voice. "I don't want you to get in trouble, Kevan."

Kevan stared at her, his mouth gaping, stunned.

Shawn relaxed his posture and held out a pair of keys. "Here, son. When you are done, meet me in the projection booth. I have been assigned to keep an eye on that ghost woman from The Mystical Order and some bratty little girl who punched your uncle. After the film starts, Vile must be out here with the car club to begin the second phase of the test ... the hypnotic soundwaves."

There was a queasiness in Kevan's stomach. He had to force his arm to reach out for the keys in his father's hands, but everything about it now felt wrong.

"Good," his father said. "Now hurry." Kevan's father stormed away from them and headed for the projection booth.

Alicia grabbed onto Kevan's arm and started pulling. "Is that Fred's car?" She pointed at a rich emerald-green hardtop—very similar to a car you would have seen cruising around on Earth in the early 1950s.

"Yes," Kevan replied, his voice dull and almost lifeless.

"Just act like you're going to put me in the trunk. I have an idea."

When they got to the back of Fred's car, Kevan held the keys out, studying them gloomily. "What's the plan?"

Alicia smiled painfully as the guy she assumed was Fred waved at her a little too enthusiastically. "Open the trunk." She swallowed back all fear. She had to remember Kathy, Marilyn, and Bethany. She had to focus on being brave and overcoming any doubt she had in herself. Relying on Kevan, who didn't seem to know what side he stood with, was going to be a risk—a big risk. "My brother has pizza. He's here with my mom in a black sports utility type of vehicle."

"Okay," Kevan looked confused as he opened the trunk.

"He always gets his pizza from a place called Goobers," she explained. "He loves that place because they always give out lots of extra parmesan cheese with every order. My brother loves the stuff."

Kevan recoiled at the thought of it. "Gross. Why are you telling me this? I hate parmesan cheese."

Alicia leaned into the trunk, swinging one leg over and then the other, then she ducked her head inside so Fred couldn't see her. "Kathy and I still have our cell phones. I'm going to text my brother to let him know what you're wearing. You're going to have to meet up with him," she said with determination before holding out her hand. "Quick, give me the keys to your dad's car. I'm going to run into the trees until it's safe enough for me to let Kathy out."

# Chapter 26

Kevan couldn't help looking back over his shoulder as he walked in between cars. He had to keep watching out for his father, or worse, his uncle. They were expecting him to head straight back to the projection booth after locking Kathy and Alicia inside the trunks of cars. But Kathy and Alicia were not locked inside of anything. He'd let Alicia take the keys to his father's car, then watched as she darted off into the nearby trees. And now, Kevan was looking for a large black vehicle that had Alicia's brother inside it—a brother armed with parmesan cheese.

A loud buzz and a pop sound from a set of loud speakers startled everyone in the parking area. Then, a deep voice with an accent said, *"Welcome students and families of Sinatra Middle School! Movie night is finally here!"*

A loud applause came from all around. Kevan frantically turned to his left, then to his right, searching for any vehicle that matched the one Alicia had so vaguely described.

*"If you will get back to your cars, we will start the movie ... oh ... yes, right. The movie is being presented by the Sinatra Student Council ...,"* There was a pause as some of the students cheered and whistled, *"... and The Piranhas Car Club."* More applause followed by silence.

Kevan was rushing around the parking area, looking into as many windows as he could along the way.

*"It is now time,"* the announcer said dramatically. *"Prepare yourselves ... and please pay close attention ... to Condemned Vampire Cookout!"*

A black-and-white film began to appear on the large screen as everyone erupted into applause again. Kevan tried to duck down a bit, not wanting to be in the way, but also not wanting to be seen by his uncle or his father if either of them was watching from inside the projection booth. Then, a window rolled down next to Kevan's head.

"Hello," a little voice said in a most adult-like manner. "You must be Kevan."

"Yes," Kevan answered, surprised at how young the boy looked. "Are you Alicia's brother?"

"Why, yes. I am."

"Uh … Okay. She told me that you really like," Kevan had difficulty saying it, "parmesan cheese."

"Yes, I do," Jimmy confirmed in a most serious, somber tone. "And Alicia told me that—"

"Jimmy?" a woman's voice interrupted from the front seat. "Is that one of Ally's friends? Can you ask him where she is?"

"Mommy! I'm busy!"

"Ask him where Ally is. Her pizza is already cold."

Jimmy scrunched his face and growled angrily. "Here," he said to Kevan, pushing his arm out the window. There were several square-shaped packets in his hand.

Kevan squirmed. He also felt a bit faint.

"What's wrong?" Jimmy asked.

"Is that … the cheese? I don't like parmesan cheese."

"Yes, it's cheese! Ally said you wanted my cheese packets!"

Kevan unzipped the inside pocket of his leather jacket and stood on the tips of his shoes. "Here," he said, forcing the pocket open and pulling it up to the window, "just put them all in here. As many as you can. I'm in a hurry."

Jimmy leaned out the window and stuffed as many parmesan cheese packets as possible into

Kevan's jacket while Kevan turned his head away, utterly repulsed. Kevan did his best to remain composed, not to seem too put off or afraid of the little packets of aged, powdery cheese. So he closed his eyes and held his breath.

"Jimmy?! What are you doing?" Alicia's mom asked.

"I'm putting cheese in this kid's pocket, Mom! He hates cheese!"

"Then why are you doing that to him?! Leave that boy alone!"

When Kevan didn't feel any more cheese packets being shoved into his jacket, he opened his eyes — instantly regretting it. Only six rows back was his Uncle Vilester, standing near the front of the projection room, staring straight at him. Kevan gasped, zipped his pocket shut, and stepped away from the window. Jimmy was so busy arguing with his mother that he didn't even notice Kevan leave.

Kevan didn't know what to do or which way to go. His uncle only stared and pointed a long finger at him. He then slowly turned his wrist upward and curled the finger toward himself. In Kevan's mind, the words, "Come here," rang inside his head.

"Yes, sir," Kevan said quietly.

Sir Vilester Ghoulingheart then scanned the perimeter of the drive-in theater, checking on the cars from his car club, making sure they were parked in the exact formation he had planned. He smiled contently and nodded at the drivers of three cars in particular, one at a time, each of them perfectly spaced apart ... at an exact, triangulated distance that had been so carefully calculated for this very night ...

Sir Ghoulingheart looked down at his nephew disapprovingly as he approached. "You're late."

"I-I'm sorry, sir."

"That's alright, Kevan." Sir Ghoulingheart pointed at the ground next to him. "Stand here, next to me. Take a look out there ... at all the cars. Do you see what I see?"

Kevan stood where his uncle asked him to, even though standing so close to his uncle frightened him. "No, sir. I don't know what I'm supposed to see."

"None of these humans are paying attention to my film. They're too busy talking and texting and eating their horrible snacks," Ghoulingheart answered in anger. "But you see, I knew this would happen. So I'm going to force them to pay attention. I'm going to force them to see and hear the messages I had carefully programmed into this film."

Kevan then watched, feeling as helpless as he'd ever felt, as his uncle raised his arm into the air, his cape flowing in the wind, and then brought it back down sharply, pointing a finger at one of the hot rods to his right. The driver instantly turned on his engine, revving it loudly. Sir Ghoulingheart tilted his chin back, inhaling the crisp night air, and then pointed the very same finger at another hot rod parked to his left. The alert driver switched on his engine and flashed a smile at Ghoulingheart.

There was now an odd hum in the air. Low and subtle, it could be felt like a faint tickle at first, but it was increasing, getting stronger. Kevan knew that something wasn't right about it. He didn't trust the sinister look on his uncle's face ... and then he realized ... *This is part of it. This is part of the plan. The sound waves!*

Kevan scanned the parking area—each and every person was now perfectly still, frozen in place like mannequins (all except the vampires, of course). Even the people at the concession stands and the ones crowded around the restrooms ... not a single person was moving. And what frightened Kevan the most, was the horrible expressions on their faces as they stared blankly at the movie screen.

"Uncle Vilester?" Kevan asked in a shaky voice. "What's happening? Why is everyone stuck like that?"

Vilester smiled. "Don't you see? Your uncle is conducting an orchestra. But instead of musical instruments, I am using the perfectly crafted sounds of engines and exhaust pipes. It's hypnotizing them."

On Kevan's face was a look of shock.

"You can feel it, can't you?"

Kevan carefully reached into his jacket, feeling for the zipper on the inside pocket, and did his best to push back any fear.

His uncle then eyed another car parked toward the front, just at the right side of the movie screen, this one resembling something from the 1930s but sort of other-worldly and more unusual. It was painted gold and glittered in silver flake. It had an exaggerated, curvy exterior. "Wait until the third engine is on." He cackled and snorted. "Then the humans will absorb and understand everything the film tells them! Hidden messages will be hidden no longer! Vampires will never be feared or ridiculed again! We will be respected, looked up to, and we will qualify for entry into any car show we wish! The universe, and its many trophies, will be ours again!"

"Or," Kevan pointed out, "you will damage the humans' brains!"

Vilester frowned like a pouty child. "Yes. Or *that*." But then he quickly recovered with a smile, raising his arm into the air again and saying in a dark, sadistic voice, "Let's find out!"

"NO!" Kevan yelled. He pulled out a packet of parmesan cheese from his pocket and ran toward the hot rod to the right.

"Where are you going?!" his uncle yelled.

Kevan didn't answer. Instead, he tore the top off the square packet of cheese, turning his nose away from it as he did, and headed straight for the car's driver. Kevan stopped abruptly at the side of the car. "Turn it off, or I'll cheese you!"

The driver's eyes widened as he studied the packet in Kevan's hands. "You're gonna cheese me with a paper square?" he asked sarcastically. "Come on, kid. Get outta here."

"There's parmesan cheese inside this thing!"

In the background, he could hear his uncle calling for him in extreme anger. "KEVAN!"

The driver of the hot rod smirked at him. "They keep cheese inside little squares? Yeah right, kid. I'm busy here and your uncle's callin' for you. Go play games somewheres else."

Kevan pushed in the sides of the packet, making the opening wider, and flicked the packet's contents into the driver's face. "I warned you!"

The driver screamed and released his foot from the gas pedal. As the vampire placed his hands over his face, Kevan reached across him and pulled the keys from the ignition.

"Hey! Ahhhug!" the driver yelled, rocking back and forth in pain, unable to see what was happening around him. "What are you doing?!"

The commotion attracted the attention of other vampires posing as members of The Piranhas. They turned to stare at Kevan, trying to figure out what was going on.

"Help!" the driver cried out. "Somebody stop him! Somebody tell Sir Ghoulingheart!"

*Oh no!* Kevan thought in a panic. He frantically turned from left to right, seeing the surprised looks on the faces of fellow vampires, but not knowing which way to run—until he saw, out of the corner of his eye, an arm waving at him. It was Alicia, hiding behind a tree, far enough outside the parking area to not be noticed.

And then he heard a deep, dark extremely angry voice coming from behind him, getting closer as it bellowed into the night, "Kevan Von

Ghoulingheart!" It was his uncle. "What are you doing?! You are ruining my plans! Get over here this instant!"

Kevan dropped the half-empty cheese packet to the ground and ran toward the trees, dodging in between bumpers and fenders. He could hear his uncle's heavy footsteps and knew how difficult it would be to escape him. It wouldn't matter how fast Kevan could run, or how crafty he could be at hiding, his uncle's senses were phenomenal and, quite literally, out of this world. He'd be caught within minutes, seconds maybe. Knowing this, Kevan rushed for the trees with a heavy heart and a feeling of hopelessness.

Sir Ghoulingheart stopped next to the car with the cheesed driver inside and glared disapprovingly. He then stared into the trees, squinting his eyes with such hatred that a vein at the side of his head seemed to protrude just a little too far. Sir Ghoulingheart took a step forward but then stopped as he heard a light, crispy sound under his shoes. He looked down, lifted his foot, and grimaced. "What is *that*?"

The driver of the hot rod rubbed his puffy red eyes and answered with a scratchy voice, "It's parmesan cheese. They keep it inside squares on this planet, sir."

Sir Ghoulingheart could hardly contain the rage he felt inside. "Turn that car back on!"

"I can't, sir," the driver replied with a whimper. "Kevan took the keys!"

Kathy and Alicia had each grabbed onto one of Kevan's arms and proceeded to pull him through the trees, guiding him toward the back of the theater. "We have to sneak behind the projection booth to get to the other side of the parking area," Kathy explained. "We have to get to the other car so we can shut it off!"

"Why? What happened when the first car stopped?" Kevan asked. "Are people still hypnotized?"

"They still look sleepy," Alicia answered. "They don't look normal. Something's still happening to them."

"And what about you two?" Kevan realized that the two girls seemed perfectly fine and as alert as ever. "Why aren't you two hypnotized?"

"I don't know," Kathy answered. "Maybe the sound waves have to hit each other in a certain direction. Maybe you have to be in between the two cars to be entranced by the sounds coming from them." She paused for a moment to scan the parking area, hoping her father was okay, seeing

Mr. Walsh leaving a concession stand with a hotdog and a drink in his hands, but he was frozen in place, staring straight ahead into nothingness.

"And there's a third car, too," Kevan told them.

"What do you mean?" Alicia asked as they reached a group of the trees near the projection booth. They looked across and behind the building, scoping out their way to the other side.

"My uncle was about to signal a third car," Kevan explained quietly. "It's at the front near the movie screen. When all three cars are on at the same time, the people in the audience will be able to see and hear the secret messages in the film. And they won't be able to look away."

"Messages meant to brainwash humans," Kathy added.

Kevan gulped. "Unless the experiment fails and the sound waves don't do what they're supposed to."

Both girls looked at Kevan, waiting for him to continue.

"In that case, there might be no brains left at all."

The girls thought about it until Alicia replied, "Ewww. My mom and brother are out there!"

Kathy pushed the thought of such a failed

experiment out of her head. "You stopped the first car. People might still be a little zoned out, but so far, your uncle's plan isn't working. Maybe if we can just get to the second car …"

"But this is just a test," Kevan told them. "He's determined to do this. Failing tonight will only prepare him better for next time. And next time, he won't fail."

"He's right," Alicia agreed. "What can we do? How can we stop him from ever doing this again?"

Kathy's face was filled with determination. "We have to get Marilyn out of that projection booth."

"How?" Kevan asked.

"Kevan," Kathy began, "you're dad's in there watching Marilyn and Beth. I'm sorry, but you're going to have to cheese him."

But before Kevan had a chance to think about, or to disagree with Kathy's suggestion, a large pair of hands reached down and clutched onto the backs of both Kevan's and Kathy's necks. Another pair of hands, hands that smelled like parmesan cheese, seized Alicia by the shoulders.

"You won't be cheesing anyone ever again, dear nephew," an angry voice said. A very, very, very angry voice indeed.

# Chapter 27

Kathy felt a little unsettled standing so close to a vampire. The projection room wasn't very large. Some people would be tempted to call it cozy. And they were all sort of crowded into it: Kathy, Alicia, Kevan, Bethany, Marilyn, Sir Ghoulingheart, Kevan's father Shawn, the driver with the red, irritated face, and in the corner, a sleeping projectionist. They each looked around awkwardly at one another.

While Sir Ghoulingheart glared at Kathy and Alicia with extreme contempt, Kathy had plenty of time to think about why she was so frightened of him. She thought on it and realized that perhaps she felt so uncomfortable standing next to this particular vampire because he was an adult vampire. He even wore a long black cape. It wasn't anything at all like standing next to Kevan. Kevan was like a regular guy with regular clothes and a great smile. He had a nice sort of walk that made him seem cool and confident. Not that she studied the way Kevan walked or thought he was cute or anything ... adult vampires were just different than Kevan. That's all.

When Sir Ghoulingheart finally stopped directing his hateful stares at the girls, he turned to his nephew Kevan. There was fury in his eyes. "Why are you doing this to me, Kevan?" And then he held out his hand. "Give me the keys."

"No." His voice quivered.

Sir Ghoulingheart nodded at his brother Shawn. "Don't make me take them from you by force. If you don't give them to me, I will begin the process of having you banned from Vashmirain, and you will never be allowed to return home."

Kevan's father stepped in behind his son to place a firm hand on his arm. Intimidated by his brother, Shawn said nothing. He could feel the intense anxiety coming from his son, but had to focus and remain faithful to his brother.

Marilyn scowled at Sir Ghoulingheart. "Kevan will have a home with The Order. I'll make sure of that."

A slight smile appeared on Kevan's face, angering his uncle even more.

"You are a traitor, Kevan!" Ghoulingheart declared. "You have betrayed your own people!"

"No! *You* have!" Kevan yelled back defiantly.

In Sir Ghoulingheart's eyes was extreme shock and surprise. In fact, everyone in the room now stared at Kevan expectantly. And for a few seconds, the only sounds that could be heard were the film projector as it softly clicked and turned behind them, the mummer of movie voices, and the faint snoring from the man scrunched up in the corner — still completely unaware of what was happening around him.

Kevan felt a surge of confidence. He shook his father's hand from his shoulder. "You are the one that has deceived our people. I have stood up for them … with the help of my new friends."

"How can you say such things?" his uncle hissed.

"This thing you call a test can destroy people!"

Ghoulingheart rolled his dark eyes, annoyed. "That's why it's called a test."

"But don't you see?" Kevan asked. "It'll make things worse! You can't force people to see things your way. You have to show them, make them believe in you."

"I *am* showing them. I'm showing them in a movie."

"No," Kevan shook his head. "You're forcing them to see the things you want them to see.

You're hypnotizing them with sound waves and hidden messages. There has to be another way to do this. Think about it, Vilester. If any of these people get hurt because your experiment goes wrong, and you mess up their brains, our reputations will be ruined."

Sir Ghoulingheart took a step back, the look on his face changing, thinking about what his nephew was saying to him.

"I promise you, Vilester. I am trying to help my people. My people are vampires ... *and* humans."

Sir Ghoulingheart looked at his brother, not in anger, but in sadness. And he said softly, "You told him."

Shawn sighed. "Yes."

Marilyn and the girls looked at each other in surprise.

Kevan knew this was his chance. "There has to be another way to help improve the vampire reputation," he suggested. He felt more confident than before, and he could see that his uncle was actually willing to listen to him. "Maybe we could try something safer. You know, something that doesn't involve brainwashing or deception?"

"Yes!" Kathy jumped in to say. "We could work together!" Excited about the idea, she turned to read Marilyn's reaction. "Right, Marilyn? Isn't there something we could do to help them? So other people around the universe aren't so afraid of vampires?"

Marilyn hesitated. Everyone in the crowded room stared at her. "Well," she began cautiously, "when The Order has a safety message or an important news report that others in the universe or other dimensions need to hear about, we film something called a Universal Public Service Message. It's like a commercial that gets sent out to several media outlets."

Kathy could barely contain her excitement. "That's perfect! We could make a film right here on Earth, showing everyone getting along and eating candy together!" She looked at Kevan. "We'll show everyone that they can be sweet and nice, and that they won't bite you or anything, even if you have a really nice neck. Everyone will see how awesome vampires are." She then looked back at Sir Ghoulingheart. "Well, *some* of them."

Sir Ghoulingheart frowned disappointedly.

"Wait wait wait," Alicia said with her hands in the air. "You mean to tell me that we could've resolved this whole thing with some everybody-get-along kind of commercial thing?"

They all looked to Sir Ghoulingheart for an answer.

He shrugged his shoulders. "I suppose so. Sorry. I guess we should have thought things through a little more." His face felt hot with embarrassment. "Please accept my apologies. I will do whatever I can to make things right. And I promise to buy each of you a candy bar *and* a soda as a show of goodwill. Would that be acceptable?"

Kevan and the girls giggled.

"A king-sized candy bar would be great," Bethany answered for them. "I accept your apology, sir."

Marilyn nodded with uncertainty and gazed into the parking area. What she saw brought some comfort to her—people were talking and laughing. Children were running around in between cars, enjoying themselves. And the vampires, although many of them had their arms crossed, looking quite annoyed, were sitting peacefully inside their vehicles, waiting for their leader's next command. "Will you make things right again, Vilester?"

"Yes, of course!" he quickly answered.

"You'll bring back the real Piranhas, unharmed, and return Alicia's and Bethany's dads back to normal?"

"Yes, but Alicia's father ... he was already so very strange when I met him—"

"Hey!" Alicia interrupted.

243

"Sorry. I will buy you, Miss Alicia, an extra candy bar. Candy bars fix everything!"

Alicia smiled, and Kathy nudged her with her elbow. "Looks like our sleepover's back on."

Marilyn inhaled a deep breath. "I think we can make things right again. Everyone in the audience only saw a low-budget B-movie? They didn't see or hear any secret messages, Vilester?"

"No," Ghoulingheart answered sincerely. "Kevan made sure of that."

Marilyn smiled at Kevan, grateful for his swift thinking and courageous actions. "The video sounds like a great idea, Kathy. But we have to be careful not to let it get into the hands of anyone on Earth. It would instantly go viral, all over the Internet." She turned to Shawn and Vilester. "I think the video, if done tastefully enough, will help in your efforts to quality for the car events you have been so eager to be a part of again. And as far as a wider distribution goes, I'll have to speak to The Order about that … but I know what would help them in making their decision."

"What?" asked Sir Ghoulingheart. "Anything we can do to help, Ms. Preston. Anything we can do to take back the selfishness of our actions."

Marilyn smiled warmly at Kevan, and even though she was transparent, the brilliance of her smile brought a simple kind of calmness into the room. "This young man here wishes to join a chapter of The Order. He wants to help people, people of all kinds. We have many lost ghosts in need of direction, and many ghouls and goblins in want of assistance and a kind ear that will listen to their troubles. Cryptids in hiding seek out a way to stay safe and unseen, and even vampires sometimes need, shall we say, a little helping hand in making the right decisions."

Vilester and Shawn Ghoulingheart blushed a little.

"Would you reconsider allowing Kevan to submit his application? I would volunteer to help train him myself."

Sir Ghoulingheart eyed his brother Shawn for only seconds before having to turn away from him as tears began to well up in his eyes.

"Are you all right, Vile?" Shawn asked before choking up with emotion.

"Yes," he sniffled. "Some of that parmesan cheese must have floated into my eyes. But never mind that … I think Kevan should join The Order. He would fit in quite nicely. Don't you agree, brother?"

Shawn gazed lovingly at his son. "Yes, I do. He's made me prouder than any parent could ever be, and he stood up for what he believed in. I am the luckiest vampire dad in the universe."

One week later

On Alicia's cell phone was a series of videos. Some of them short, some longer, some taken at school during lunch, or taken at the mall with Kathy while documenting their shopping experiences. But one video in particular looked strikingly different. This one had an odd-looking man in a black cape at the beginning of it. His face was pale, his eyes quite striking … and he was sitting next to Kathy in a restaurant booth, picking at a piece of cake.

"Just point the camera at me," Kathy insisted.

To say that the man seated next to Kathy looked uncomfortable would be an understatement. His dark beady eyes darted everywhere as he asked quietly, "Is this really how Earth commercials are made? They make them with cell phones?" the man asked in a thick, mysterious accent.

"It's more like an infomercial," Alicia clarified from behind the cell phone. "Have you heard of those?"

"No," the man answered. "Do they film those

with cell phones, too?"

"Uh," Alicia began, "due to budget constraints, the cell phone will have to do. Kathy and I have plenty of great video editing apps that will make all of this look very professional."

The man put his head into his hands.

"No, you need to sit up straight," Kathy said while attempting to prop the man's head up. "You need to do Earth things. That's what the cake is for. Are you ready?"

Alicia placed three fingers in front of the phone's camera and proceeded to count backward, "Three, two, one ... action!"

"Hello, people of the universe and multi-verses. My name is Kathy Preston. And I have a message for you about my friend here, Sir Vilester Ghoulingheart." Kathy turned to nod at the man next to her, cueing him to speak.

"Hello."

"You see, this man and his people have been misunderstood for many years." Kathy turned to him again. "How are you enjoying your cake, Vilester?"

The man took a bite of the cake and grimaced slightly. "Mmm. It's very good. Sort of."

"That's very interesting, Vilester, because that cake has garlic in it."

The man smiled weakly at her. "Oh. That was nice of you. Thank you for doing that."

Kathy looked into the camera with a serious look on her face. "You see? Garlic has no effect on this vampire. That's because he is just a regular undead guy. In fact, we walked here with him to this café … in the sun. Also, there were many people that we encountered along the way, all of them had very nice necks. Vilester didn't bite a single one of them."

"I prefer Sir Ghoulingheart instead of 'undead guy.' It sounds more proper—"

"So the next time you see a vampire, whether it be on the street, in a movie, or at a car show … please, take the time to understand that they don't want to harm you. They just want to work on hot rods and win trophies. Right, Vile?"

"I like motorcycles, too."

Kathy put her arm around the man, and he very obviously resisted the urge to recoil. "Vampires are pretty neat. In fact, I hope to visit the vampire planet of Vashmirain someday in hopes to learn more about them."

"Uh … you do?" the man asked, looking a bit worried. "Will you warn, I mean, email us first?"

"Ally, zoom in," Kathy said. "As a citizen of Earth, all I ask is that you give vampires a chance.

They don't want to bite you. They just want to show you their fancy cars and not brainwash people."

"Kathy," Alicia interjected, "don't say anything about brainwashing. It doesn't sound right."

"Fine. Edit it out," she said in a huff. "I'm doing all of this without a script, you know."

The man looked into the camera. "Are we finished yet?"

"I think there should be some hugging at the end," Alicia suggested with a giggle, causing the camera to wobble in her hands.

"No thanks," the man said.

"Yeah, count me out of that, too." Kathy laughed.

"Oh! I know," Alicia yelped. "Turn into a bat! That would make a great ending. I'll add music to it!"

The man's pale face flushed with color. "Oh, come on. That old trick? I don't want to look like I'm showing off or anything ..."

"Please please please!" Kathy begged.

"Okay. But only for a few seconds, girls."

And with a wink and a sudden poof, the man changed into a little black bat, hovering in the air above the booth as Alicia and Kathy cheered with delight, and some man a few booths behind them gasped and inhaled a bite of his marmalade toast the wrong way at the sight of it.

To the disappointment of Alicia's little brother Jimmy, the video abruptly ended. He held Alicia's cell phone in his hands, his mouth gaping open, and his eyes set very wide. "Ally had cake with a vampire guy from another planet and didn't invite me?!" Jimmy looked toward his dresser, fuming. "Does that sound fair to you?"

"Look, kid," a short, big-headed alien with large black eyes said to him with disinterest. He had a group of action figures lined up on top of Jimmy's dresser, ready to send them off into an imaginary battle. "I already told you … vampires don't exist."

## THE END …?

Creepy Vampire Drive-in